"You seem to know what it takes to cheer me up."

"Distraction, but it's too far to drive here all the time. I'll have to think of other ways to preoccupy you more often." He grinned, his index finger tapping his cheek. "How about…"

She took advantage of his pause. "How about you being my distraction?" Her pulse skipped as the thought grew and the words slipped out.

He looked surprised but it faded to a wide smile. "That's the best idea I've heard in a long time. I'm happy to do the job, ma'am. I promise to be one big distraction from now on."

She loved his smile. "I hope you keep your promise." He opened the car door and she slipped inside, aware that telling him about her mother had lifted a burden from her shoulders. She'd never told a living soul, and he'd listened without judgment and made her feel less guilty than she'd felt in years.

Books by Gail Gaymer Martin

Love Inspired

*Loving Treasures
*Loving Hearts
 Easter Blessings
    "The Butterfly Garden"
 The Harvest
    "All Good Gifts"
*Loving Ways
*Loving Care
 Adam's Promise
*Loving Promises
*Loving Feelings
*Loving Tenderness
†In His Eyes
†With Christmas in His Heart
†In His Dreams
†Family in His Heart
 Dad in Training

 Groom in Training
 Bride in Training
**A Dad of His Own
**A Family of Their Own
 Christmas Gifts
    "Small Town Christmas"
**A Dream of His Own
 Her Valentine Hero
 The Firefighter's New Family
 Rescued by the Firefighter

Steeple Hill Books

The Christmas Kite
Finding Christmas
That Christmas Feeling
   "Christmas Moon"

*Loving
†Michigan Islands
**Dreams Come True

GAIL GAYMER MARTIN

A former counselor and educator, I've enjoyed this career as an author, writing women's fiction, romance and romantic suspense since my first book in 1998, with this being my fifty-second novel. My books have been honored with many national awards, and I have more than three and a half million books in print. I've also authored *Writing the Christian Romance,* released by Writers Digest Books. A cofounder of American Christian Fiction Writers, I'm also a member of the ACFW Great Lakes Chapter, RWA and three RWA chapters. When not writing, I enjoy traveling, speaking at churches and libraries, and presenting writing workshops across the country. Music is another love, and I spend many hours involved in singing as a soloist, praise leader and choir member at my church, where I also play handbells and handchimes. I sing with one of the finest Christian chorales in Michigan, the Detroit Lutheran Singers. I'm a lifelong resident of Michigan and live with my husband, Bob, in the Detroit suburbs. Visit my website at www.gailgaymermartin.com, or write to me at P.O. Box 760063, Lathrup Village, MI 48076, or at gail@gailgaymermartin.com. I enjoy hearing from readers.

Rescued
by the Firefighter

Gail Gaymer Martin

HHARLEQUIN® LOVE INSPIRED®

Recycling programs
for this product may
not exist in your area.

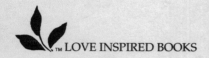

™ LOVE INSPIRED BOOKS

ISBN-13: 978-0-373-81758-0

RESCUED BY THE FIREFIGHTER

Copyright © 2014 by Gail Gaymer Martin

www.Harlequin.com

Printed in U.S.A.

But if we walk in the light, as he is in the light,
we have fellowship with one another,
and the blood of Jesus, his Son,
purifies us from all sin.
—*1 John* 1:7

Thanks to my Facebook group, Readers of
Gail Gaymer Martin's Books, for their support,
ideas, helpful comments and wonderful reviews.
I also thank two firefighters who provided excellent
details to guide me in being realistic in my
portrayal, Chuck Harrelson of Colorado and
Tim Kohlbeck of Wisconsin. If I erred, I can't blame
them. Thanks to my agent, Chip MacGregor, and as
always my deepest thanks and love to my husband,
Bob. Without his support, proofreading and patience
(especially that), I wouldn't be the writer I am today.

Chapter One

Paula Reynolds looked down the church aisle and watched the guests being seated. She felt as jittery as the bride. She checked her watch and studied her cousin. "How are you doing?"

"Nervous...and anxious." Ashley sent her a playful grin. "Today my life changes forever."

Paula gave a nod, unable to voice the words that were caught in her throat. Forever had been her cousin's hopes when she married Adam, but fate had had other plans. Ashley had endured a bitter blow when Adam had died in Afghanistan, leaving her and a baby son he'd never met. The memory overwhelmed Paula.

She moved closer, trying to avoid crushing Ashley's wedding gown, and gave her a hug. "I'm so happy for you."

Ashley's eyes grew misty. "I know you are." She held Paula in her embrace and gave her a squeeze. "Don't wrinkle that gorgeous dress." She eased out of Ashley's arms and shifted back toward the doorway to wait for the music to signal her down the aisle. A bridesmaid. She'd never have believed it six months ago.

Images swept through her, filling her with longing. She wished she'd had siblings of her own, but she smiled now, enjoying the friendship of her two cousins, who'd hurried to her side when they'd learned of her mother's death. They'd opened their arms as if she were another sister. With their recent closeness, Ashley had asked her to be a bride's attendant. Make-believe sister or not, her cousins' love touched her more than anything had in years.

Silly how she'd worried that Ashley felt obligated to ask her, and to give Ashley an out, she'd insisted the honor wasn't necessary. Thankfully, her cousin's determination won over, and when Paula accepted, her heart had tripped and the ripple of pleasure surprised her.

Ashley had not only insisted she participate in the wedding, but the bride-to-be solicited her sister, Neely, and her to help select an appropriate wedding dress for a widow. They found the lovely gown Ashley wore today, a calf-length cream-colored dress with three-quarter sleeves and scooped neckline with a formfitting waist that fell in soft folds over Ashley's trim figure. Today her cousin looked gorgeous as she stood close to her father, who waited to walk her down the aisle.

Ashley beckoned to her again, concern on her face.

Paula hurried to her side. "What is it?"

"Is something wrong? You were looking at me, and I thought—"

"I was admiring your dress." She chuckled. "We all loved it the moment we saw it."

Tension vanished from Ashley's face. "Look at you. I've never seen you in a gown. You're beautiful."

No one had called her beautiful before. She lowered her gaze to the pastel coral dress she wore, a color in autumn leaves floating from the trees outside the church. "Thanks. I love it."

Images of fall flashed through her mind, a time of rejuvenation as the summer foliage took a rest anticipating a rebirth in spring. That was what she wanted for herself. Her lingering memories needed to be buried so her life could sprout new hope. Though her optimism didn't always deaden her difficult past, little by little she'd seen the sun. She had her cousins to thank for that.

"I love this time of year."

Ashley's voice cut through her thoughts. "I know. It's when Devon and I settled in as a couple following my accident." Her eyes grew misty. "I'll never forget wakening that day with a gorgeous angel—"

"Angel?"

"Okay, it was Devon, but he was like an angel. He was peering at me and holding poor little Joey, who was so frightened." She blinked tears from her eyes. "He saved me in so many ways. He heard

Joey crying and then saw the downed tree and came running."

"He's that kind of man, Ash, a gift after all you went through." Her cousin's remembrance filled her heart. She couldn't picture herself being rescued by anyone.

Ashley glanced at her dad and then her watch. "I wonder what's taking so long." She lifted concerned eyes to Paula. "Is Devon up front yet?"

Paula stepped back to the doorway and shook her head. "He'll be there." She drew back to her stance near the wall, her eyes on the chancel. The ceremony should have started five minutes earlier, but that was life, too. Things didn't always happen as planned.

With Ashley's past heartbreak in her mind, Paula wished this time her cousin's marriage would last a lifetime, the kind of union she'd dreamed about for years. Though still single at thirty-five, Paula would still enjoy Ashley's wedding and sometimes let her thoughts consider marriage to a wonderful man—whether it would happen or not.

Organ music diverted her from her thoughts. The men were filing out from somewhere, and she gave Ashley a thumbs-up. Her heart skipped as she began her trek down the aisle. Ahead, Devon, his brother, Derek, and his firefighter friend Clint Donatelli observed her slow pace to the front. Though uncomfortable with all eyes on her, she managed to concentrate on the happiness she'd found living in Ferndale, welcomed by her cousins and Uncle Fred, who had graciously invited her to stay with him until she found her own place. She'd do that one day. Soon, she hoped. But that precluded finding a job and finalizing her mother's estate. Too much to think about today.

The scent of the flowers drew her back, and she gazed at the men, still observing her snail-paced journey. She'd grown fond of Devon with his sturdy frame and not one ounce of fat—just solid muscle. So was his friend Clint, handsome in his dark suit, tall and lean, his Italian heritage reflected in his dark brown hair flecked with gray and classic features. But the stereotypical Italian image ended when it came to his deep blue eyes.

Clint was her idea of a perfect man, but those dreams, as much as she loved them, seemed out of reach. Her relationships with men had always ended in disappointment. Sometimes worse.

Drawing her focus from Clint, she concentrated on her long, slow trek. When she reached her place at the front, she turned to admire Neely gliding down the aisle, wearing a hunter-green dress shimmering in the light from the windows and carrying a bouquet the same as hers, a blend of autumn flowers—golden black-eyed Susans, orange roses, flame calla lilies, green hydrangea blossoms and burnt-orange hypericum berries.

The music grew louder, introducing the bridal fanfare. The guests rose and faced the entrance as

Ashley moved forward on her father's arm. Startled by her tender feelings, Paula blinked to clear her blurred vision as tears sneaked from her eyes and formed rivulets down her cheeks. With everyone's attention on Ashley, she brushed away the moisture, digging deep to shoo away her emotion. This kind of reaction had been unwelcome in her life. Whatever bad happened, she'd always buried her emotions, unwilling to give way to something as useless as tears.

Ashley nudged her sister with the bridal bouquet, and Neely grasped it as Ashley and Devon exchanged vows. The familiar words swept over her, leaving her with questions. How could anyone promise to love someone forever, to be faithful and true to them in sickness and health until death? Her parents' lives had provided no example of love or faithfulness. Her own experiences left her empty and frustrated.

Instead of wasting time thinking about the past, she needed to focus on the future, just as Ashley was experiencing today. She studied Ashley's and Devon's faces, seeing what she'd never seen in her own reflection. Even Neely's gaze toward her husband, Jonny, seated in the second row, was filled with a kind of beauty that she'd always considered part of a fairy tale—Cinderella or Sleeping Beauty awakened with a kiss.

Her own experiences identified more with the Beauty facing the Beast but without the loving tears that turned the beast into a handsome prince. Instead of tears, her emotion had turned to ice. The man who'd promised her a lifetime of happiness but never offered her a ring had left her with a wounded heart and an empty purse. A longtime relationship filled with promises as cold as a winter ice storm.

But today the moisture in her eyes unleashed more positive thoughts. Could the new door that had opened with her uncle's family unlock her heart and her trust, as well? Life didn't always offer such choices. Yet here she was in a new environment surrounded by a supportive family.

As gentle as a breeze, the wedding kiss ended, and Ashley reached for her bouquet. On Devon's arm, she smiled at the guests as they moved down the aisle to greet them in the narthex before they left for the hall. Neely latched arms with Devon's brother, and Clint stepped to Paula's side. Her pulse skipped when he locked his arm to hers, noting his strength beneath the dark suit that complemented his over-six-foot frame.

Her reaction frustrated her, but she managed a smile and ignored her pulse, which was galloping like an unbridled mare. Somewhere in her subconscious, an alert sounded. Vic had been out of her life for almost three years, but she still knew better than to even think romantic thoughts. Not again. She'd fallen prey before. Reacting to someone she barely knew put her on dangerous ground. Yet, despite her wise counsel, Clint melted the ice in her veins and sent warmth coursing through her. Her mental struggle floated away on the organ music. Today was about Ashley's wedding and not some kind of ridiculous fairy-tale moment.

Clint guided Paula down the aisle, surprised at her response when he'd taken her arm as the others had done. He didn't think of her as timid, but he'd felt her guard mount at his touch. When they'd met for the ceremony rehearsal, she'd stood back, observing before she became involved. Beneath her quiet demeanor, he sensed her mind snapping. And that was what did it. She'd aroused his interest. No one had done that for years. He'd chalked it up to her vulnerability. Firefighters had a penchant for helping people in trouble. Though she smiled and chatted once she'd warmed up, beneath her smile, he sensed something deeper churning inside a locked trunk. Yet she couldn't hide those lovely eyes, the color of caramel, which seemed to match her long, wavy hair.

He almost shook his head at his concocted analysis. The woman was new to town. Some people took longer to get comfortable. He'd spoken a little to her and sensed she wasn't a churchgoer. Yet faith seemed a stronghold for her family. It was what had helped Ashley through the loss of her young husband, a man who'd never seen his newborn child other than in photographs. Clint's chest constricted, wondering how he might feel being denied that amazing privilege of seeing a child created from the love of a man and woman.

A smidgen of envy wheedled into his consciousness. Nothing good ever came of envy. Not one thing. Envy caused displeasure and longing, sometimes resentment. Envy thwarted what lay ahead and signaled lack of trust in the Lord. He dismissed this negative thought and pinpointed a new goal.

He hoped the occasion would lower Paula's guard. He would enjoy learning more about her, and he juggled ideas how to make it happen. His discouragement grew while standing in the reception line. Seeming on edge, she appeared to know few of her relatives and spent most of her time explaining who she was by mentioning her mother, Dorothy, who'd died recently. If she wasn't comfortable with her relatives, what hope did he—a stranger—have?

The last guest greeted them before heading for the reception hall, but he'd been warned they had to stick around for photos. He studied Paula's expression and took a chance. "Do you mind posing for pictures?"

"Do you?"

He jerked his head back, an instinctive reaction to her abrupt response. "Not really."

"Me, neither."

Her short response held a playful tone, and she made the cutest face, her nose wrinkled while the corner of her mouth curved to a faint grin. He plowed ahead. "Do you think we can escape?"

"If you know Ashley, you already have the answer."

He liked her snappy responses. "Then we'd better give in and follow them."

She released a dramatic sigh and hooked her arm through his, different from her earlier reaction, which made him curious. They followed the others to stand beneath the lovely cross where the stained-glass windows puddled brilliant colors on the carpet.

"Ready to plaster on a smile?" He gave her arm a squeeze.

"Ready as I'll ever be. How about you?"

Making a move, he slipped his arm behind her back and guided her toward the photographer. "Same here."

She considered him a moment and, to his pleasure, she didn't draw back.

Rather than scaring her off, he left well enough alone. He'd acted like a naive schoolboy, noticing for the first time that girls were different. Today the same awareness slithered down his spine. It was natural. Four years had passed since being with a woman who attracted him.

He'd pretty much steered clear of women until now, since Elise had walked out of his life without one backward glance. Why she'd waited so long, so close to their wedding day, he'd never know. No wonder he'd been confused. Perhaps one day he would figure out what he'd done wrong.

Trying to be subtle, he studied Paula from a

peripheral view. She didn't seem ready for anything either, so who was to say he and Paula couldn't be friends? Friendship served both involved. Fun, laughter, companionship. Maybe that was all he needed—time to adjust to a woman's companionship. It might be easier than he thought.

Paula touched his arm, an inquiring expression on her face. "Come back to planet earth. The photographer is giving you a look."

So was she, and he liked it.

Music filled the hall as Paula entered with Clint at her side. She spotted the deejay near the dance floor, a middle-aged man who'd probably been entertaining wedding parties for years.

"I think our seats are over there." Clint beckoned her to follow, and behind him she admired his physique as he guided her to the bridal table. At first, she'd felt trapped, and it made no sense. Clint had been pleasant company, polite and tempting her smile to appear. For too long, she hadn't smiled much, and, since coming to stay with her uncle Fred, she'd found herself chuckling at his amusing comments and her cousins' easy wit. Today she discovered the same kind of playfulness in Clint.

Though his comments didn't draw out belly laughs, they tickled her. Sometimes he echoed her own terse responses, teasing innuendos that he tossed out on the fly. Nothing at all like Vic. When she allowed herself to face the truth, the "trap" was different. She'd felt knotted in a web but not a spider's dinner, instead a maze luring her to follow a path different than she'd experienced before. Though tempted by the adventure, a thought struck her. Had Ashley put Clint up to entertaining her? Maybe he was the one who really was trapped.

Irritation bristled down her back. Why dwell on what had been? Somehow she had to stop comparing Clint to Vic. Better she let the present cover the ashes of her past. Beauty from ashes.

"Are you all right? You're quiet." Clint pulled out her chair and waited for her to sit.

She managed a pleasant look. "Thinking."

He slid the chair beneath her and studied her a moment, his dark blue eyes gliding across her features and causing unfamiliar sensations to roll through her belly. "Problems?"

The single word caught her unguarded. "Not really. I was…I was trying to recall where I'd heard the phrase beauty from ashes."

"Scripture." He sat beside her as other attendants ambled to the bridal table. "I'm not good at telling you where in the Bible." He shrugged. "But I know it's there."

"Thanks." He'd impressed her, and what he'd said made sense. Only God could take ashes and make them beautiful. Sometimes she thought about church and faith, realizing life would have been different if she'd had something…someone to lean on.

Clint had strength to lift a tree. Definitely strong enough to lean on. Still, he wasn't God.

"I'm guessing there's more on your mind."

Her head snapped upward, nearly giving her whiplash. He'd shifted the chair toward her, and in her preoccupation, she hadn't noticed.

"I didn't mean to impinge on your thoughts. Sometimes I can't stop myself from probing." He rested his hand on her shoulder. "I suppose that's the firefighter in me. We need the facts. Details. Saving property and lives need quick thinking."

"But I don't need rescuing, so you don't need facts." She managed a smile.

He shrugged. "Most of us do at one time or another."

"I guess we all like details. Tell me about you." Her knack for reversing the conversation gave her control, and she could avoid talking about herself.

"Firefighter...but then you know that. Single." He held up his left hand and spread his fingers.

No ring, but she'd known that. "How have you escaped so many women looking for a husband?" Instead of a smile at her teasing comment, he couldn't hide his frown before managing a grin.

"Lucky, I guess."

Cover. She'd used the same technique. She turned in the chair, her knees brushing his. "You're kidding, I know."

He gave her a crooked grin and shrugged, but his eyes probed hers a moment before he looked away.

"Truth is I was engaged once, but it ended before the wedding. I'm glad, since I don't believe in divorce."

The statement reminded her of her earlier thoughts in the church. How could two people promise a lifetime of love and faithfulness when so much of the world didn't seem to value it at all? "That's your religious belief?"

"Yes and no. It's biblical, but it's also a gut feeling. I'd only marry if I knew deep in my soul this person loved me with all her heart, and she trusted that I felt the same. Too many things change in life, and I don't think marriage should be one of them. We need to hang on to a few constants. Faith is one of those I cling to."

The word *cling* gave her pause. Her faith fluctuated from one day to the next. "You're lucky."

"I'm blessed." A frown slipped to his face. "Are you saying you're not a believer?"

His expression made her reluctant to speak. "I wasn't raised in any faith."

Instead of drawing back, he eased forward, as if longing to ask about her beliefs, but silverware tinkled against china and glass, and Paula turned to see what caused the commotion. She spotted Devon leaning forward to kiss Ashley as the guests cheered and tittered. She'd forgotten that old kiss-the-bride tradition.

Toasts to the bride and the table blessing ended and, grateful for the break in conversation, Paula eased back in the chair as the waitstaff delivered food to the table and the meal began. Conversation buzzed through the room, and though she and Clint talked, the topics were general and unimportant. The issue of faith seemed to hover above them.

As dishes were cleared, the music began. Clint rose and extended his hand. "Care to dance?"

She hadn't danced in years and the idea of being in a man's arms—Clint's arms—appealed to her. Yet again the question rose. Did he feel obliged to dance with her? Despite her questions, she followed him to the dance floor, her own longing taking precedence. The swish of the silky fabric against her legs awoke her feminine self, a persona she'd ignored the past few years.

On the dance floor, he pulled her close, his arms holding her fast yet with a tenderness that eased her. He glided effortlessly, their feet moving in sync, their bodies swaying to the rhythm of the music, a love song that fit the occasion. Others had joined them, and Paula felt less conspicuous. The closeness to Clint filled her with longing, the desire to go back in time and relive her life differently.

She recognized a good man when she saw one, and Clint fit the image. Her thoughts turned to Ashley and Devon's marriage, a day of joy and happiness for two people she hoped would enjoy a forever life together. Though Vic had dampened her dream for a while, she felt a determination to move forward. The new environment, new friends, new experiences gave her the opportunity to find happiness.

When she looked up, Clint was studying her, his beguiling eyes engrossed as he observed her. Beneath her hand, his powerful frame reflected not only his physical strength but his solid character. He would make a wonderful husband for someone. Her pulse tripped, sending her mind into unfamiliar places.

As Devon and Ashley twirled past, he caught Clint's attention, and when the song ended, Clint guided her to their table. "I'll be back in a moment. I think the groom wants me for something." He tilted his head toward Devon and hurried off.

The intrusion caused her to wonder what was up, but a few moments later, Ashley broke away from her task of greeting people and slipped to her side. Ashley sent her a coy grin as she sank into the empty chair. "You and Clint seem to be getting along very well."

Paula's heart skipped again, and she struggled to keep color from rising to her cheeks. "He's being a gentleman. I think he knows I'm a stranger here… even among relatives. I haven't seen these people in years, and they don't really know me."

Ashley rested her hand on Paula's. "I think it's more than that." Her grin needed no words. "But Clint is a gentleman. That's for sure."

"What do you mean by 'more than that'?" Although she understood, she wanted to hear what Ashley had to say.

"He finds you enjoyable company. That's what I see." Hope lit Ashley's face.

"He makes me laugh. Nothing seemed funny while I cared for my mother." She pictured the pain her mother had suffered. It didn't leave room for frivolity. "It's been a long time since my life has seemed…" Words escaped her, and she delved into her vocabulary to find the right way to explain. "Normal, I guess."

"It's nice to see both you and Clint comfortable with each other." Ashley shook her head, a nostalgic look washing over her face. "Did I ever tell you when I met Clint?"

She shook her head, anxious to hear something new about him.

"When I was pinned under the tree, Devon stood over me with Joey in his arms, but another voice slipped beneath my dazed confusion. Clint. I could tell he was nice just by the way he spoke to me."

She agreed, though she wished Ashley had more to tell.

Ashley shivered. "Even though I met Devon, when I think of that day I freeze. The storm came up so quickly, and I ran out to move Joey's wagon and put my car in the garage. A couple of minutes, I thought, so I'd left him sleeping on the sofa." She shook her head. "That was a lesson learned. I'll never leave Joey alone for a second now. He woke when the tree fell against the house and came outside looking for me. In my rush, I'd left the side door open. He couldn't find me. Devon said he was crying when he heard him."

"That's scary." She'd heard Ashley relive those horrible moments more than once. But out of bad came good. "It's wonderful, too, Ash. Joey and Devon found you buried under the limbs. Today proves how great that day was."

Her cousin chuckled. "I know, but I keep reliving it. Devon told me how Joey kept calling to me, trying to wake me up."

She patted Ashley's hand. "Devon is a real hero."

"He is. A true hero." Her mind wandered a moment before she continued, "Clint's the same kind of guy. A good man who's still single." Ashley arched her brow. "You know he hasn't dated much at all, from what Devon says."

"I didn't know." She'd sensed it, though, but Ashley's reference triggered more questions. "He mentioned his broken engagement. Do you know what happened?"

"Devon doesn't say much, but from what I understand it was totally unexpected, and it left Clint wondering what he'd done to end their relationship."

Paula's chest tightened, recalling the same unwelcome experience she'd also encountered. "Perhaps he did nothing wrong at all. He's totally thoughtful and nice." She pictured his endearing smile and quirky comments. Someone that sweet and good-natured had to be easy to be with. "His fiancée may have been the one with the problem."

Ashley nodded. "You know, I think you're right. Now all you have to do is help Clint see that."

"Me?"

Her cousin rose with a playful expression, yet beneath it was sincerity.

"Why me?"

"No specific reason. I just think you'd be the woman to do that." Ashley squeezed Paula's shoulder. "I need to get back to our guests, but I wanted to tell you that I'm happy you've met Clint." She spun around, gave her a crooked smile and moved toward the dining tables.

Paula gazed ahead, looking past the tables until she spotted Clint. Why would Ashley think she could do anything for anyone? The only thing on her mind at the moment was to get a job and find a house to move into. She couldn't take advantage of her uncle for too long. He'd invited her to stay until she got settled. *Settled* was the key word.

The thought smacked the truth. She'd never been settled. Not really.

Chapter Two

"How was the honeymoon?" Clint gave Devon a wink as he strolled to his locker to slip into his work gear.

Devon arched his eyebrow, a silly taunt on his face. "Were you worried?"

"Not one bit. I knew you were in good hands." Clint gave him a thumbs-up. "Ashley can handle you." More than a week had passed since the wedding, and while he'd missed seeing Devon at the fire station, he'd found Paula on his mind more than his good friend.

"You're right, Ashley's amazing." Devon turned to face him. "In all seriousness, the longer I've known her the more I admire her and the more I love her."

Clint's chest tightened, picturing Paula and what he liked about her. He'd be happy to see the end of his worries about trusting again so he could take steps to form a friendship with her. After the incident with Elise, his motto had become "Get hurt once but not twice."

"Seriously, though, the honeymoon was wonderful. I had never been on a cruise, and the Caribbean is beautiful—scenery and summer weather." He took an imaginary key and locked his lips. "But enough yakking. I'll have photos and you can see for yourself."

"Can't wait."

Devon's expression let Clint know he'd recognized his playful sarcasm. But for once, Devon was wrong. Clint had never cruised, either, and wouldn't unless he had someone with him to share the experience. He really wanted to see the photos.

Devon's locker door clanged shut, and Clint's mind snapped back to his task. As he slipped into his work gear, he reflected on what he'd really wanted to know from Devon. Had he seen Paula since he'd been back or had Ashley said anything about Paula mentioning him?

Though he'd had a great time with her and thought she'd enjoyed his company, too, he'd hesitated asking to see her again. His hesitation made him want to kick himself. But Paula made him uncertain. She seemed to have built a wall and stepped behind it. If he moved too fast, he could easily find the barricade a permanent shield.

And then he posed a question to himself. What did he want from her? A relationship hadn't been a priority for years. Involvement sometimes led to marriage, and he wasn't positive he wanted to marry. At thirty-seven, he liked being stuck in his own ways, and marriage meant making changes, adjusting to someone else's likes and dislikes.

Clint closed his locker and strode in for roll call before digesting and discussing the information passed on by the previous shift. Devon, the on-duty lieutenant, listed the tasks each of the crew would be responsible for, and when he finished, Clint headed into the equipment room to assess the gear he might need during the day.

As he checked off the equipment assigned to him, Devon appeared at his side. "We're having a little party Friday night for the wedding attendants and a few others. All the women want to see our gifts and the photos, so we thought it would be fun. I hope you can come. We'll have pizza. It's casual."

As if he'd been invited to an audience with Queen Elizabeth, Clint felt his pulse take off in a gallop. He monitored his zealous reactions. "Sounds great. I'll be there."

Devon squeezed his arm and moved on to his duties while Clint stood a moment to deal with the unbelievable reaction he'd experienced, particularly assuming Paula would be there. If he couldn't control his emotions better than that he needed to go into hiding. He'd prided himself on being a staunch, capable firefighter who could handle a life-and-death job every day. Emotions were locked tight so his mind could make the quick decisions that each dire situation needed.

What had happened to that skill today?

He shook his head and turned his mind on the training session and the next tour of the firehouse he would lead. School would be out soon, and one of the treats for elementary children was visiting the fire station. This duty shone as one of his favorites. He'd always loved kids and, sometimes, never having children of his own hurt worse than the day his marriage plans died.

Though his heart had healed, he couldn't help thinking about Elise. What had driven her away? What had changed her mind about their marriage?

Dumb questions, and what difference did the answers make? He needed closure, he sensed, like people did with a shocking death. Those who grieved always pondered what had happened or what they could have done to make a difference.

He had looked back on the situation and had come to the realization she'd fallen for someone else. Probably the jerk in her office she talked about so much. He'd been married, and at the time, he'd dismissed the possibility. But marriage didn't mean as much to some people as it did to him. Vows were made and God blessed marriages. To him, marriage meant forever.

Paula crumpled into one of her uncle's easy chairs and rubbed her temples. She'd had another job interview, which again left her with a hopeless feeling. Though she had the numerous skills they'd listed, she didn't have experience with their software program. Then, another strike against her appeared to be her newness to the area. When they looked at her résumé, they noticed she hadn't worked a few months before her mother died. She'd been her caregiver. Work had been impossible.

Most businesses looked for someone with stick-to-itiveness and experience, but if no one would give her a chance, how could she get the experience? Another one of these conundrums that made no sense but seemed to be prevalent in the world of business.

The back door opened, and Paula pulled up her shoulders. Though five foot nine, today she felt a lot shorter. She needed to lift her head and face her uncle with confidence. He always wanted details of her job hunt, and she wanted to sound positive even though she wasn't.

Ashley swung around the archway, and when she saw Paula instead of her uncle, a grin flew to her face.

"Home from the hunt?" Ashley said.

"The fox found a hiding place today."

"No luck?" Ashley sank onto the sofa. "You'll find something. I'm confident. I'm keeping my eyes and ears open, and I'm sure something will come your way."

Paula nodded, managing an upbeat expression. "I know. Job hunting takes time."

The side door closed, and her uncle's voice sailed into the room. "A job well done."

She had no idea what he meant, but she hoped it had nothing to do with her employment status.

He ambled into the living room and stood near the archway. "Did she tell you?"

Paula looked at him and then turned back to Ashley, not sure who he meant.

"Dad, you're more excited than I am." She grinned at Paula. "I decided to sell my house. Dad helped me make sense out of what I really knew was best but what was hard for me to do."

"Selling the house." Paula nodded, understanding her quandary. "I know it holds lots of memories, Ash. Good memories." Her own mother's home came to mind. That house held no memories she wanted to preserve. "But you're making new memories now, and it's best to let it go."

"You've all made sense. I thought renting it would work, but then Dad reminded me of the difficulties in renting a residence—maintenance, repairs and bad tenants. It hardly seems worth it even though the house is only down the street and Devon would have helped, but—"

"It would be asking a lot of him to keep two houses in good order. When would you two have time for fun?" Paula looked past her uncle, noticing the two children were missing. "Where are Joey and Kaylee?"

"Neely wanted to take them to the park." Her

mouth curved to a full grin. "I'm so happy Neely's expecting. She and Jon wanted a baby from day one, and now she'll have her own little Joey or Kaylee to spoil."

Though her cousins' happiness made her smile, part of her envied Ashley and Devon's big steps into marriage plus becoming a parent to each other's child, especially now that Kaylee's troubled mother had died from an overdose. It had been hard on Kaylee, but her awareness of her mother's illness and unhappiness had softened the sad situation.

Marriage had not made Paula's list of desires, so the question of being a parent rarely entered her mind, but when it did, it sometimes stopped her cold, asking herself if she could be a good parent without having a role model. One thing she knew. Love was the key to so many things in life, and how could she not show love to a child? Ashley's love for Joey and Kaylee, Devon's daughter, guided her cousin's every step, and Devon had an amazing natural knack for being a thoughtful and loving father to both children. They had become her parental role models. Late in her life to learn, yes, but she knew no one better.

Ashley had grown silent a moment, a frown settling on her face, and Paula didn't understand the problem. Paula turned to her uncle, wondering if he had something to clue her in.

Finally, Ashley came back to life. "Sorry. I know this is the right thing to do, but I love that house and it's hard to let go. Believe me, it's not just my memories of Adam. It's where I realized that I had the strength to stand up under pressure, where I learned to be a loving single mother and still hold a job, and where I awakened beneath the tree branches one day and looked into Devon's face, a neighbor I'd seen but never met. That day changed my life."

Paula brushed moisture from her eyes, no longer trying to hide it. "You're right, Ash. The house has a wealth of amazing memories. One day, I hope to have a…" Before she could finish her sentence, an idea struck her. She needed a place to live, and owning a house would provide a sense of permanence to a possible employer, but more than that she loved Ashley's comfortable house and felt certain it had more than enough space for her.

When she refocused, Ashley's curious look caused her to confess her idea. "I have a thought."

"A good thought?" Ashley's tentative response made Paula grin.

"Very good, I think. My mother left me everything, and I need a house. I don't want to go back to Roscommon. It's a dead end for me there. Do you think—"

Ashley jumped from the sofa and flew to her side, where she plopped on the chair arm. "Paula, that's an amazing idea. Perfect. You'd be close to us, and I would know the new owner is someone who cares about the memories and, even better, is someone we love." She turned toward Uncle Fred. "What do you think, Dad?"

"You don't need my approval, and I think it's a good idea, except..." He turned his gaze from Ashley to her. "Would you feel restricted to make the house your own, Paula? If you'll feel restrained, or Ashley..." He faced her. "If you'll resent Paula redecorating or even renovating, then it's not a good idea. You both need to consider that."

Paula knew how she felt, but her uncle's question put the possibility into a new perspective. "That's something we have to consider, and Ash, you need to talk it over with Devon." Though the possibility thrilled her, a problem lay ahead, and the reality drowned her excitement. "But face it, I don't know what I'm talking about. I don't have a job yet. I need to put a clamp on my enthusiasm. I can't make payments without work, and I'm not sure how long it will take to settle the estate. Mom had savings, but I've used some of it to live on these past weeks." The situation crushed her spirit. She wasn't a kid facing life for the first time. She knew hopes were one thing. Reality was another.

"But Paula, we can—"

"Ashley, I couldn't get a mortgage right now." Her excitement died a quiet death. "I don't even have a down payment without nearly wiping out my mother's savings, and I don't know how long it will take to sell her house. I hope it's soon, but I have no guarantee."

Ashley shook her head. "We can work that out, and we're not in a hurry. A sale by owner doesn't restrict us resolving that issue, either. You're right, though. I'll talk with Devon, but I'm sure he'll have no reservations." She leaned over and kissed Paula's cheek. "I love the idea, and even thinking about it, I'm relieved."

Ashley's positive attitude should have lifted her spirit, but a woman of her age didn't go off the deep end. Her old resentment returned. She'd allowed Vic too much leeway, and while she wasn't looking, her own savings had dwindled to little. He'd walked away, leaving her in his dust with nothing but empty hopes and an empty bank account. How could she have been so stupid?

"Hold on, Ash. Really, I need to take time. I'd love the house, but I have to use common sense. I contacted a Realtor and mother's house should be on the market now. I'll call them and check the status."

Ashley's excitement faded. "Okay, but we'll still give it thought and I'll talk to Devon and see if he has any ideas."

Ideas were fine, but she had to keep her head. Having a home of her own tempted her to take chances, but getting a grip on her overexuberance, wisdom needed to come first. She'd been stupid once. Let it only be once.

They gave each other a playful handshake, and though it was lighthearted, Paula faced the depth of the decision. Problems could be resolved, but they took thought and time.

Ashley hugged her and gave her dad a peck on the cheek, then headed to her car while Paula sat and pondered the rash decision she'd wanted to make. Since moving from her mother's home and being on her own, she'd only lived in an apartment or flat, and though she liked the possibility of owning a home, it tied her down and forced her into a commitment to stay there. Still, since coming to Ferndale, she'd wanted a place to call home, a real home, and she liked the idea of being around Clint. He'd lingered in her mind no matter how much she tried to push him out. She hoped they could become friends.

His tender smile washed over her, the crinkles around his eyes, the few silvery strands that highlighted his dark hair, the flex of his strong arms as he moved. Her past relationships broke into her thoughts and she blocked the images. Men appeared in and out of her life with no heart and no depth. She'd begun to think most men were like that. Her father had been, as far as she knew. He'd walked out on them, apparently with no looking back. Vic had kept the apartment and sent her packing. But Devon and Clint, even her uncle Fred, proved that some men were different. Some had the capacity to care and love…really love.

That had been her problem. She'd made rotten

decisions because she wanted to be loved and had no idea how to make it happen.

And it never did.

Clint parked on the street and made his way to Devon's front door. Before he rang the bell, the door opened, and Ashley greeted him. "Good timing. I just put out some appetizers." She motioned him inside. "We'll order pizza a little later."

"Sounds great." He stepped through the door, his gaze sweeping the living room and dining room. He recognized Devon's brother and a few of the others, but he didn't see Paula. His breath hitched as he wrestled a frown from his face.

"Make yourself at home." Ashley swung her arm toward the dining room, where he saw food spread on the table.

Disappointed, he headed toward the appetizers. He'd come to the party, and he'd make the best of it.

"Clint."

He paused and turned her way.

"Some of the guests are in the backyard. We've been blessed with a bit of Indian summer." She grinned. "Drinks are there, too."

Hoping she hadn't seen his reaction, he called a thanks over his shoulder and inspected the hors d'oeuvres, his stomach knotted with anticipation. He slipped some veggies and dip onto a paper plate, took a couple of taco chips and guacamole and pushed open the backdoor, trying to focus on getting a cola. But the bluff ended there. His true purpose was to see Paula.

And he saw her when he stepped outside. She sat in a canvas folding chair, the sun glinting streaks of gold in her hair, today the color of caramel. Beside her, he recognized one of Ashley's friends, and he hesitated to interrupt. Instead, he found the cooler loaded with soft drinks and, on the picnic table, he spotted pitchers of iced tea and lemonade and made his decision.

While he scooped ice cubes into a plastic cup, his gaze swept the guests, hoping to spot a firefighter or someone else he knew. But no one passed by that he'd consider a friend. Maybe he'd missed someone inside.

As he reached for the lemonade pitcher, a piping voice calling his name stopped him. When he turned, he saw Kaylee bounding toward him with Joey on her heels. He set down his glass and shifted his attention to the little girl. Her arms stretched upward, and he grasped her, spinning her around while avoiding wiping out the table.

She giggled, and noting Joey's envious look, he set her on the ground and crouched beside the two cute kids. "How you doing, slugger?" He tousled Joey's head and gave him a squeeze.

"Good." Joey's loving grin sank into his heart. "Kaylee's my sister now."

She giggled and put her arm around his back. "He lives in Daddy's house and not down the street."

"I heard, and I saw you both at the wedding. You looked so beautiful, Kaylee, and Joey, I've never seen anyone more handsome in a tuxedo."

The boy's face beamed. "Handsome like my new daddy."

"Exactly." He hated to dismiss the kids. Their loving nature stretched his heart and made him yearn for the same kind of joy, watching his own little boy or girl—maybe both or more—grow up to be adults he could be proud of, but that joy hadn't happened. He didn't know if it ever would. His attention slipped to Paula before he managed to refocus.

"Joey. Kaylee." Ashley's voice drew nearer. "You're supposed to grab something to drink and then go back inside and play the game you set up."

Hangdog looks spread across their faces.

Ashley patted their heads. "Your auntie Neely isn't going to stay long, and she's—"

"'Cuz of her big belly with the baby."

Kaylee's information caused Ashley and him to muzzle their chuckles. Clint gave Ashley a wink and both kids a hug before they did as they were told.

She moved on, and before he finished pouring his drink, the woman Paula had been talking with passed by, and he noticed Paula alone, an empty chair beside her. He grasped the paper plate in one hand, his drink in the other, and ambled her way, hoping she looked pleased when she saw him. His wish came true.

"Do you mind?" He tilted his head toward the chair.

"Not at all." She moved an unsteady folding tray closer to his chair. "It's been a while."

Too long, as far as he was concerned. "It has been." He settled into the chair.

"I noticed you over there with the kids." She swung her hand in the direction of the drinks table.

He loved that she'd noticed him. "They told me they're brother and sister now. They were glowing. Great it hasn't been a problem."

"Ashley and Devon did a good job preparing them." She fell into silence.

He joined her, remaining silent for a moment until he could respond to her first comment. It had been a while since he'd seen her. It's not what he wanted, but his lack of confidence with women had taken hold. He braced himself for what he needed to do. Make progress. "I heard through the grapevine—" he shifted his elbow toward Devon heading his way "—you might buy Ashley's house."

"That's the rumor." She grinned but said no more.

Before they could continue, Devon stuck out his hand for a shake. "Glad you made it. I invited a couple of guys from the station, but they're not here yet." He winked at Paula. "I can tell that's no problem since you know this lady. You see the crew all the time." Devon chuckled. "And she's better-looking."

Being subtle was not Devon's forte. Even without his friend's encouragement and his attempt to monitor his emotions, Clint's heart responded. "Absolutely." He managed a smile that he hoped looked natural. Being relaxed with a woman, especially one he liked, escaped him. It seemed harder work than double shift at the station.

"I'll let you two enjoy your conversation." Devon gave Clint's shoulder a squeeze, winked at Paula and turned to leave but slowed before pivoting back to them. "Oops, I forgot." He slipped a photo packet from his shirt pocket. "I'm supposed to be letting people take a look if they want." He gave Clint a poke in the shoulder. "I know you were interested."

He held out the envelope, and Clint grasped it, avoiding comment.

Devon paused. "You ought to take a cruise like this, Clint. But you don't want to go alone." He gave him another wink and strolled away.

Clint sat a moment clutching the photos. "He's not very subtle, is he?"

Paula chuckled and took the envelope from his hand.

He wished he could dodge Devon's obvious comment and suspected Paula was thinking the same. Everything between them was so new and needed time, nurturing in a way. Still, how could he handle a relationship that seemed like work and yet held a promise that drew him forward?

Paula opened the envelope and pulled out the stack of photos. He followed along as they viewed the shots glowing with beautiful sandy beaches, sunsets spreading across the ocean seascape, hammocks between palm trees and a candlelight dinner, Ashley and Devon dressed in their finest.

"Lovely." Paula's voice sounded airy as she turned to him. "I've never seen a place like this."

"Me, neither." So many words bunched into his mind, but only thoughts he had to keep to himself. They barely knew each other, and yet she seemed a longtime friend.

They sat in silence again until Paula cleared her throat. "Getting back to your question about the house."

Weighted thoughts lifted from his shoulders.

"I'm seesawing over what to do about the house. Devon and Ashley are encouraging me and offering leeway on the deal, but I'm using common sense."

He wondered what she meant by leeway but let it slide. "It's a really nice place, but that is a big step. Why not live in your mother's home?"

As soon as she heard him, she scowled. "Her house is in Roscommon, partway up north. I don't have any reason…anything to keep me there."

She'd covered her tracks on the comment, but he could guess what she avoided saying. Being reminded that her mother had lived in Roscom-

mon, he was glad she'd decided to sell the house.
In Ferndale she had family and, he hoped, a growing friendship with him.

"I know buying a house is a big step. Ashley's
house fits my needs, and it's in this area." She
glanced away and pressed her lips together.

He could see she was fighting temptation. She
wanted the house, and he could only pray she held
on until buying wasn't financially risky.

"But I can't be rash."

It was too late to cover his relieved sigh. "Good
thinking."

A faint frown flickered on her face. "My finances
aren't quite resolved yet. Some money was left in
the estate, but to buy the house, I need a job as well
as the income from the sale of mother's property."

He recognized the problem, knowing the value
of homes had dropped in the past few years and
selling was at a snail's pace. But Roscommon. Was
there work in that small town to motivate people to
buy? His practical nature let questions seep into his
mind, but he turned off the flow before he put his
foot in this mouth again. Paula didn't seem to welcome his financial viewpoint. "Any hope of finding a buyer?"

"Good news is the house already has a bid on it,
and the Realtor said it looks good. It'll be a relief
to get rid of that problem."

Her references to *relief* and *problem* aroused his
curiosity again, but her reference to a job sounded

right to him. Maybe she had a good head on her shoulders. "I hope it works out." From her expression, he'd obviously disappointed her. She'd expected his enthusiasm, but his parents' way had been solid. Until the money was in hand, the offer was only a dream.

She nodded and fell silent again.

Questions dug into his mind, ones his parents would ask about budgeting and saving money, but the probing could end their amiable conversation. He headed for the safest topic. "Do you have siblings?"

She shook her head. "I'm surprised my parents had me." As the words left her, she grew silent, her expression reflecting her shock that she'd said that much.

He sat glued to the seat, his lips pressed together, unable to think of anything safe to say.

"I'm sorry, Clint. I'm sure that sounded crude, and I'm surprised I said it."

"Maybe you needed to."

Paula tilted her head as if weighing his comment. "You may be right. I tend to hold in things until they explode." Looking uneasy, her attention drifted toward a couple of new guests who'd arrived. She dragged in a lengthy breath. "I should explain, I suppose."

He didn't try to stop her. Instead, he grasped his drink and leaned back in the chair, giving her time to decide what she wanted to say. Her expression created an unexpected ache. He'd suspected she buried things she didn't want to deal with or think about. Her comment proved he'd been right.

"I was never close to my parents. My dad split when I was still young. I hardly remember him, and my mom led a guarded life, one that didn't involve me. I don't think she ever said 'I love you' to anyone."

His chest constricted, air escaping his lungs. Everyone needed to be loved. He'd grown up hearing those words from his parents, and he knew that Jesus loved him. The childhood song swept through his mind. "I'm sorry, Paula. The words 'I love you' are precious."

She nodded without looking at him. "I can't believe I'm telling you all of this." She looked away for a moment.

"I like getting to know you."

"Really?"

He nodded, aching from the look on her face. "My life wasn't perfect, either. Not by a long shot."

She studied him as if to make sure he meant what he said. "Thanks." She raised her shoulders.

He waited.

Her shoulders slumped as if carrying the weight of her past.

"I'm here, Paula." He tied down the other words longing to be spoken.

Her head turned toward him like a weather vane in a faint breeze.

When her eyes met his, he spoke those bottled-up words. "And I'm listening."

A wash of questioning rippled across her face before she took a deep breath. "I moved away from home as soon as I could. Took some college classes and worked a job to help pay for an apartment I shared with a couple of girls. When I finished my associate degree, I got a full-time job and took courses to work on a bachelor's degree, but I never finished." She shrugged. "It's difficult working and going to school. I was dead tired all the time. I decided to put the dream to bed for a while." She shifted and focused on him. "As life goes, I never went back to college."

"That happens. I started classes at Michigan State, but then got the firefighter bug. College isn't necessary for the job, although it can help someone move up in the ranks. I plunged ahead, passed the written, physical and medical exams, and then earned my certification as an EMT."

"I'm impressed." She lifted her plastic cup and took a sip.

"Don't be. It's a job someone has to do, but I love it. Saving lives and helping people in trouble gives me an opportunity to do what I believe is important. You know the old saying, 'What would Jesus do?'"

Her head inched upward. "Should I be honest?"

His eyebrows raised, and he forced them down. "Please."

"I don't know what Jesus would do. That's another part of life I missed out on."

"Religious training?"

"My mother wasn't a believer, I suspect. No Sunday school or church. Nothing."

"But that doesn't mean you can't be a believer. That's something in the heart, not always in the home."

Her expression darkened.

Concerned, he leaned forward. "I hope I didn't offend you. I just meant that my faith deepened as life went on. I was born into a faith-filled family so I saw it in action, but it didn't deepen until I experienced life and saw faith acted out each day."

"I suppose." She stared into the distance for a moment, then continued. "I'm surprised Neely and Ashley have a religious foundation. Their mother and mine were sisters. Maybe if I'd had that kind of upbringing, my life would have been different."

"Hard to say why siblings aren't always the same." The urge to encourage her to study and grow in faith stirred through him, but he feared the results. "Maybe their dad was the influence."

A faint grin etched her mouth. "Probably was. Uncle Fred's down-to-earth, funny and very thoughtful. He's quite a character."

"He is. I get a kick out of—"

"Pizza." The word rang out as Devon came through the back door, holding a number of Jet's Pizza boxes, while Ashley made room on the picnic table. "Time to eat."

Eating was the last thing Clint wanted to do. Paula had opened up, spilling out some of the hurts and situations that had molded her into the person he wanted to know better. But as others headed toward the table, Paula rose, and he followed, letting the subject drop. He sensed there was much more to tell, but today he'd made a little progress in getting to know the woman who'd become the center of his thoughts. Thoughts he couldn't control. Ones that demanded attention.

Pizza restricted their conversation, leaving him with the undaunted urge to rescue Paula from the hurts and damage from the past. He sat unmoving, the desire growing in his mind. He'd rescued many from flames and other tragic situations.

But this was different. Was rescuing Paula even possible?

Chapter Three

Paula hesitated before pulling into the driveway when she spotted Devon and Clint near the garage with her uncle. If Clint hadn't noticed her and waved, she would have backed out and driven away. Today wasn't a day she wanted to talk with anyone. On top of that, when she thought of him, and it was more often than she wanted, she pictured him with Kaylee and Joey, and it charmed her. He was wonderful with them. Natural, outgoing, relaxed. He looked like a guy who knew how to be a dad. She had no idea how to be a mother and, if she tried, would she be a good one?

She'd been fighting tears for the past hour, tears she resented, and her weakened ability to control her emotions was almost too much. Everything had gone wrong, even the memory of Clint with the kids. That should have lifted her spirit. What had happened to her new lease on life?

She sat a moment, willing her pitiful tears to

dry up. Self-pity wasn't an appealing trait. No one wanted to deal with that, and she didn't want to, either. She pulled her shoulder bag from the floor where it had slipped and hoped she could sneak into the house.

As she rounded the car, her uncle Fred beckoned to her. Her heart fell as she managed a pleasant expression and headed his way, wondering what he wanted. Devon and Clint watched her traipse along the driveway though forcing each step. "What's up?"

Her uncle swung his arm toward a large pile of fireplace logs piled into a bin at the side of the garage. "We're ready for winter. Free firewood. How often does a person have that happen?"

She shrugged, having no experience with fireplaces or logs. "That must have been a good deal."

"Yep, but we had to move it today. Devon called and said a tree had fallen a few streets over, and they wanted to get rid of the wood." He clasped his son-in-law's shoulder and then flopped the other arm around Clint's. "These two men came to my rescue. I had no way to load this myself."

She managed a smile at the men. "That was really nice." She choked on the word. Nothing had seemed nice since she'd awakened, but she wanted to be happy for her uncle and his woodpile. The image caused a true grin to tug her mouth.

"We were glad to help." Devon patted her uncle's shoulder.

Clint sidled closer to her and tucked his hands into his pockets, a knowing expression on his face. "How was your day?"

The gentle tone of his voice touched her like a breeze, and words failed her. She swallowed her rising emotion and shrugged. She wanted to run rather than stand beside him whimpering, but she noticed Devon had followed Fred around the corner of the garage, and she and Clint faced each other alone.

"Something's wrong?" He shifted closer. "I see it in your eyes."

Having someone read her thoughts triggered her emotion to break free. She looked away, fighting back the lump in her throat and the pressure behind her eyes. "A little."

His arm slipped behind her and drew her closer. "No luck looking for a job?"

She tilted her head, willing her mouth to form words. "That's one of the problems, and I'm beginning to sense it's not going to happen."

Clint grasped her shoulders and turned her to face him. His midnight-blue eyes searched hers, and the dam broke. Tears slipped from her eyes and rolled down her cheeks. He glanced behind him and drew her to his chest.

That was all she needed. Sobs broke loose as her tears wet his polo shirt. She sniffed, trying to force back the ache rending her body. Foolish. That's how she felt. She'd lost control, and her disappointment had knotted into a wad of sickening self-pity. "I'm sorry, Clint. I'm being ridiculous."

"Let me be the judge of that."

"But I'm not a crier. Tears and I are strangers—were strangers—and I want it like that again."

"Really." He looked at her with question. "Why?"

"Tears are weak, and that's something I'm not." Though she said it, the words felt like a lie. Somehow she'd weakened and had turned into a pile of mush. No one liked mush, especially her.

"Even men cry, Paula."

The sincere look in his eyes gave her a start. She studied him, confused. Who was this man? Strong, confident and yet tender. The vision tripped in her mind.

Clint glanced toward the garage and then motioned toward the house door. "Can we go inside?"

She sensed he wanted privacy, and Uncle Fred didn't always know when to vanish. She led the way to the side door. They entered the kitchen, and she pulled two glasses from the cabinet. "Would you like something to drink?"

"Hold on a minute, okay?" He motioned toward the backyard. "I want to see if they're finished. The more I think of it, I'd rather we go for a ride and talk without interruption."

She knew what he meant.

He turned and hurried down the landing to the side door without giving her a chance to respond. But maybe that was good. Saying it wasn't necessary would have been dishonest. Being with Clint would be the best experience she'd had all day.

She returned one glass to the shelf, turned on the tap and filled the other. Her mouth felt dry, and she gulped the cool water, wishing away the depressing feelings that had overtaken her.

Though Clint's offer had met her need, she didn't want their first conversation since Ashley's party to be like this, but she needed to dump her worries somewhere rather than lug them with her, and Clint had volunteered. A true rescuer of many kinds.

As she set the glass in the sink, Clint returned and stood on the landing. "I hope it's okay for you to leave." He studied her a moment. "Will you go with me? You're guaranteed no interruptions."

Her usual resistance had disappeared for once. She slipped her bag over her shoulder and followed him outside.

"By the way, I told Devon and your uncle we were going out for a while. I didn't explain."

"Thanks." She felt protected with Clint. He had a way of making her feel safe.

He motioned her to go ahead and steered her toward his Jeep across the street. There, he held open the door as she alighted, and then he slipped into the driver's seat. "What about a park? The weather's great, and it won't be like this for long. We can pick up a sandwich and drink…." His eyes caught hers. "Or will that mess up dinner? I'm guessing you do the cooking for your uncle."

"True, but he has plans tonight at the seniors' center. He has a lady friend." She pictured her uncle's boyish charm when he talked about Alice. "She's from the church."

Clint pulled away from the curb as he chuckled. "You can't find a better place to meet someone."

She shriveled into the seat, and though she knew he didn't mean to make her feel ashamed, he had. Being a believer was important to him. Fleeting images skipped through her mind, pictures of her and Clint walking into church...maybe with children, but those images weren't her, and she sensed he was letting her know that if she had ideas about a relationship, she'd better forget them.

He turned onto Hilton Road and pulled into a parking spot to pick up a sub sandwich. When he stepped out, he leaned back inside. "Want to come in and see what they have?"

His church reference had saddened her. Though he didn't mean it to, she suspected he was right. For a Christian, where better to find friends? She shook her head. "No. Surprise me?"

Arching an eyebrow, he shrugged and closed the door.

If she'd gone inside, she may have been able to dismiss his comment. It wasn't necessarily a warning. He knew she hadn't grown up in a faith-filled family. As yet he hadn't rejected their friendship.

When he exited the sub shop door, he swung the bag and dangled it in the air, a silly grin on his face, and for a moment it caused her to smile. Clint could do that for her.

He slipped into the car and handed her the sack. "Now to Harding Park. It's close."

They rode in silence, her mind on him and her problems, and his mind...? She couldn't even guess.

"Wouldn't you know." He motioned toward the park as they approached.

"What's wrong?"

"Who would think. It's busy today." He pointed ahead as they turned the corner.

She spotted the problem. The few picnic tables appeared filled, and some people were playing with toddlers at the nearby swings.

"They're enjoying the last days of summer." He waved his hand again in another direction. "Soccer game going on, too. So much for being alone."

She eyed the food bag he'd handed her. "We could eat in the car."

"I have a better idea, and it's close." He followed the street around a bend and turned at the next corner onto Inman Street. "I hope you don't mind."

Before she could figure out what he meant, he pulled into a driveway.

He shifted into Park and turned off the engine. "My house. It's quiet and I have an umbrella table in the back if you prefer."

She studied the two-story yellow-sided house with white trim. A castlelike turret jutted from one side, and the porch reflected more old-world charm, with four columns supporting the roof. The architecture was enchanting and different from any home she'd noticed in the area. Intrigued by the look of the house, she pictured Clint inside.

Maybe he had an old-world charm, too. Each time they met, she noted his staunch values and ways. Old-fashioned manners of opening doors and holding chairs, niceties that had been lost by most of the men she'd known. "It's really pretty, Clint." She admired the well-kept yard and the turret—it made her feel like a queen.

He jumped out, came around to her side and opened the passenger door. "Thanks." He motioned toward the side of the house. "Let's go in back."

Though disappointed not to see the inside, she walked beside him. When she rounded the corner, a flagstone patio extended from what might be a kitchen door. A table and four chairs in deep green and a matching umbrella took most of the space. Farther left, he had two outdoor recliners sitting in the sun with a small table between them.

She settled onto a chair, and he used a napkin from the bag to brush off the tabletop that already looked clean.

"I hope you like turkey and ham with cheese." He slid a wrapped sandwich in front of her.

"It sounds good. Perfect." She folded back the paper as he set a napkin next to the wrapper. Her stomach rolled a low growl. "I didn't realize how hungry I am."

"And I bought you a lemonade. I hope you like it." She chuckled, seeing his concern.

"Doesn't everyone?"

His expression brightened as they sat in silence, unwrapping the meat-and-cheese subs thick with lettuce, tomato and cucumbers. Even a pickle peeked from beneath the multigrain crust. She took her first bite, tasting the blend of flavors, and washed it down with a sip of the lemonade, amazed she'd almost forgotten her less-than-perfect day. Keeping those thoughts to herself, they chatted about his landscaping and house, topics that drew her attention away from her earlier upset.

With her appetite sated, she managed to finish most of the sandwich before she gave up. "Thanks for suggesting this. Otherwise I would have gone inside Uncle Fred's and wallowed in my misery."

He shook his head, a half smile on his face. "I can't picture you wallowing."

"Oh, but I do. It's something new, another weakness, that's happened since my cousins encouraged me to move here after my mother died."

His grin faded. "They're nice ladies. Devon and Jon caught two good ones."

A grin slipped to her mouth. "You make them sound like fish."

His belly laugh surprised her, and she chuckled along with him. "I've always been very private, and talking about my problems is something I've never done. I've tried to understand why I'm compelled to open up to you." Though blunt, the truth had to be spoken. She wanted him to understand her struggle.

He reached across the table and slipped his hand over hers. "You don't have to tell me what's wrong. I don't mean to pry. I only thought it might—"

"I know you're not prying. I'm the one who blubbered all over your shirt." She leaned closer with her free hand and placed it on his chest. "It's dry now." Warmth rushed through her palm to her fingertips as his well-toned physique stirred beneath the knit shirt.

"If it were drenched, Paula, I wouldn't care."

His expression washed over her—kind, tender, honest—the kind of look that she'd missed with Vic. Seeing Clint's sincere ways, she should have known Vic was using her, but at the time she didn't care. When desperate, blocking reality had a value, but lately she'd begun to face the truth. She'd been hungry for love, a kind of hunger that turned lies into hopes. "Thanks. I'll keep that in mind the next time I need to cry."

"I hope you do." His eyes captured hers.

Like a cord binding them, she felt close to him, a feeling she couldn't explain. A kinship, perhaps. The silence lingered, a comfortable quiet only disturbed by a chirping bird and the breeze ruffling the shrubs nearby. "Would you like to hear about my second problem?"

"If you're ready to talk."

"The buyer for my mother's house backed off.

No sale." The words caught in her throat. "I hate to tell Devon and Ashley. They were so excited that I planned to buy the house."

He turned his head as he focused into the distance for a moment until his eyes met hers again. "Remember, it's only been on the market for a short time."

She nodded. "But I have no guarantee when it will sell. So many homes take years. They don't want to wait that long. I hate to tell Ash and Devon."

"But it's smart thinking. Waiting makes sense. You don't want to jump into something you can't handle. When it comes to finances, I…"

She brushed her knuckle across her eyes where tears had begun to form. "I'm just disappointed. I'll get over it. I always do."

"You probably don't want my opinion, but you'd be smarter to stay with Fred, even rent a small apartment, until you can make a secure move into your own house. My parents taught me to be sensible. Having savings means more than—"

She flexed her palm, not wanting to hear his lecture. "I really want that house, Clint. It's close to family. Ashley and Devon are right down the block, and—"

"You'll find another house close by when you can afford it. Never take chances when it comes to security."

Stopping Clint served as much purpose as holding back the tide. Hopeless. Still, she looked at his expression and read his meaning. "I'm like a little kid, Clint. I want things when I want them. I know a woman of my age should know that it's not the end."

His shoulders relaxed. "Definitely not the end. It's only the beginning."

The beginning. Her hopes rose again, but she pushed them aside. The man wanted a woman he'd met in church, not one who trusted a jerk like Vic, who'd knocked the stilts out from under her with his treatment. But Clint received support from his family. He had no idea what it was like to learn from making mistakes and then having to repair them.

She didn't want a lecture, but she'd learned one thing about Clint. He was a straight arrow, a man of honor, although she found herself questioning his advice. Somewhere along the way, she'd picked up some warped judgments. Maybe she could undo them. Her mind slipped back into her pre-Vic mode. She'd been far more open and trusting then, even though her life was a mess.

"You're quiet." Clint searched her face, his look reflecting his own confusion. "I didn't mean to bring you down."

She'd done that herself. "I'm questioning my judgment. Maybe I should think things through without being nestled in the family's embrace. You know?" She analyzed his expression and questioned whether he understood or not. "Sometimes I ask myself if I should stay here. I've never been dependent on anyone."

"No." His hand rose, his palm flexed.

Though his face reflected concern, his vehemence startled her. "What are you saying? I don't think you understand what we've been talking about. I have no job. No house. No assur—"

"Have you always run away from problems, Paula?"

She'd never called it running away, but maybe that's what she did. She gave a nod, assured that trying to hide reality from Clint was useless. He always read the truth in her face.

"If you've spent your lifetime running, you've given up hope. Being hopeless isn't the kind of life that makes anyone happy. How many times have I seen you laugh when you're with Fred and your cousins? The day I met you, you said things that made me chuckle. Life can be filled with joy. Fun. But you'll never find it if you don't take a chance. Stay in one place and deal with problems. Running solves nothing. Confronting does. I've run away, too, Paula, in my own way."

She tried to recall what she'd said to trigger his adamant comments. But it didn't really matter. Letting his message soak into every pore, she was nourished by the images that rose in her mind and she could only utter a truth. "I have loved it here."

"I'm not challenging you, Paula. I only want you to dig deep for the answers. Nothing comes to the surface without a willingness to dredge up the sludge and find the gold. Running stomps down character. Standing firm builds it."

She drew up her shoulders, recognizing the truth he spoke. Though his words stung, Clint had a way of stating the truth. "You're right. I know you're right, but sometimes it's easier to walk away than deal with it."

"Give it time. The house will sell, and I'm sure that Devon and Ashley won't be fazed. I guarantee."

"You are sure of yourself." She managed a grin, longing to lighten the moment.

"Firefighters have to be confident."

Though she'd never given it thought before, she would want a person who saved others to be sure-footed—even someone rescuing her. A chill shivered down her spine. Was saving her Clint's mission? Did he want to rescue her from herself? She met the questions with confusion, even disappointment.

Though she'd grappled with her feelings for him, she wanted his friendship if nothing more. At this time in her life, she needed a friend, a person who could choose to like her without feeling an obligation. She appreciated her cousins treating her like a third sister, but she was family. They really didn't have a choice.

While her mind raced with questions, Clint had risen and extended his hand. "The sun moved and we're in the shade. It's too cool for you out here. Would you like to see the inside?"

The offer intrigued her. Clint had anticipated her wish again. She needed a distraction from their serious conversation, and his awareness, his over-all thoughtfulness, calmed her. While her hand remained in his, his strength became hers. "I'd love to."

Clint's eyes blurred as he viewed the training video. He'd seen this one numerous times, yet reviewing the skills he needed to be a firefighter headed the top of his "important" list. But today his mind drifted back a few days to when he showed Paula his home. Maybe he'd been wrong to give her a tour as if he were rubbing her nose in the lack of her own place.

Her house plans and her financial situation tumbled like a house of cards. When they'd talked earlier, her attitude about finances concerned him. Though she'd captured a piece of his heart, certain aspects left him thinking. Why didn't she have savings? Yes, she'd apparently cared for her mother and perhaps had to take a leave from her job, but still…

He'd been raised to save money and budget. At first, Paula's decision to buy the house had been made without thinking it through. Her drive to own a home blanketed the need to have a solid plan to pay for it. He rubbed his neck, remembering he'd probably said too much to her, but she'd been clinging to the edge of common sense. Still, her sensitivity preceded her ability to handle a lecture. Learning to shut his mouth was a necessity, or he'd damage the new friendship they'd developed. She needed a friend, but then so did he. She'd already been through the loss of her mother and uprooting herself to Ferndale. His comments had verged on a turnoff for her. He could have uprooted their fragile friendship with his blabber—his know-it-all attitude—and he would never forgive himself.

And then he may have added fuel to the fire, not something an intelligent firefighter wanted to do. When he'd invited Paula inside, he'd been aware of her guarded reaction to things, but he'd suggested it anyway, anxious to see Paula in his home, to see how she looked in the kitchen or seated in his family room. Sometimes he pictured her there beside him. Foolish, he knew. The images troubled him at times—another conundrum—a bittersweet moment, like dreaming the impossible dreams he'd heard about in song.

He pressed his back against the less-than-comfortable chair, facing an awareness he'd had during their talk. Though he'd encouraged Paula to relate her problem, he had also understood that Paula wasn't the only one running. He hadn't felt at peace since his marriage plans had collapsed.

Life had passed him by after Elise left. He went to work, did the laundry and kept the house somewhat clean, but his social life had sunk into an abyss. He didn't want to date. Having fun seemed impossible so he stayed home. He'd even passed on going to the movies or to dinner with Devon until one day Devon put his foot down and wouldn't accept his refusal. That day began his uphill climb.

Paula needed something…someone. Perhaps encouragement to stick it out and fight for what she wanted in life rather than give up. She'd made it clear that running sometimes seemed easier than standing still and grasping for the future. But truth be told, they both needed to stop dwelling on things they couldn't change and get on with life.

Maybe Paula and he could find answers in each other. He couldn't think of anyone more lovely to heal with. As she had told him about the house sale falling through and her thoughts about moving away from Ferndale, he longed to take her in his arms and hold her. He wanted to understand the depth of her problem. Running hinted that something else caused the reaction, something more dire. It wasn't her mother's death or her lack of savings. Those were situations in her past she couldn't change. Or was she trying to run away from herself? That seemed impossible. Paula had strength that could fight off many battles. He'd seen hints of it. So what was it that nearly did her in?

His eyes flew open as the video ended. The others rose, rustling papers and sliding their chairs into place. He looked around, hoping no one had witnessed his lack of attention. Not a single person gave him any notice so he breathed a relieved sigh. As he rose, he sensed someone behind him. When he turned, he saw Devon leaning against the door frame and watching him.

Guilt skittered up his back. The man knew him too well, and he waited for the question.

"What's going on?"

"Thinking." He shrugged. "Sorry, I know I need to watch the—"

"You're seasoned, Clint. We show the videos as a review, especially for the newer guys although it helps all of us to stay on our toes."

Clint found no meaningful response, and he trailed along with Devon heading for the day room, his mind on his tasks for the shift. Before he made the turn, Devon paused and rested his hand on Clint's shoulder. "You've been spending time with Paula. I'm glad. She needs friends." Devon eyed him with obviously more on his mind. "How's it going?"

His face heated, a giveaway to the feelings he'd tried to hide, but he wasn't fooling anyone, especially Devon. "She needed to talk, and I offered to listen."

"Good excuse." Devon chuckled. "I'm happy to see you stepping out a little, pal. You've been harbored too long. Time to get the paddles working."

"She's nice. I like her, but really, she needed to talk and I—"

"Don't explain. I know." He squeezed Clint's shoulder and lowered his hand. "I'm guessing it was about the house sale falling through."

He nodded, hoping he hadn't overstepped her confidence.

"I'm sure you knew we wouldn't stop her from buying the house. A job will come, and her mother's house will sell eventually."

"That's what I told her." But he'd also told her not to buy the house until she had the finances, and not just finances but a solid savings. He fidgeted in his pocket, trying to pull out his hankie. He didn't need it, but it gave him something to do. He considered Devon a best friend, but at the moment, he felt cornered.

"Have you thought about asking her out?" Devon searched his face. "On a date, not just to talk."

"You're too nosy, pal."

"Just getting even. I remember a year or so ago, when I was getting the sly questions and winks from you prying into my visits with the 'young woman trapped under the tree.' Remember?"

Clint chuckled, his discomfort easing. "I think you quoted that verbatim."

"Close, at least." Devon gave him an elbow. "But being serious, Paula's been through a lot."

"I know a little about her family life but not much more." His anticipation grew as he wondered what Devon might know that he didn't. "How about you? Any details?"

"Paula holds things in. I'm not sure Ashley knows much more than I do." Devon glanced at his watch.

"Paula needs time to trust people. At least that's my take on it."

Clint nodded and let it drop. Even if Devon knew something, he'd probably not feel right sharing it.

"No matter what, she can use a wise, steadfast friend, and as you know, I think one Clint Donatelli can be that person with the help of a quick kick in the pants. Life is in front of you, buddy, not behind."

"Thanks for your sage advice, Mr. Cupid." Though a ripple of heat unsteadied him, he winked at Devon. "I'll take your comments under advisement."

"Good, and to help you along, Ashley has invited you over for a wild game of Sequence. Can you make it Sunday evening?"

"Never heard of the game, but Sunday night's open."

Devon grinned. "Not anymore."

Clint let Devon's lightheartedness spirit his attitude. He turned toward the day room but halted when Devon called his name.

"In case you didn't guess, Paula will be there, too."

Clint's stomach tightened. "I suspected." He raised his hand and didn't look back. All he needed was someone pushing him when he needed time to let the idea grow. At this point, the idea of a friend felt good, but he wasn't totally confident it was what he should do or what he needed. First, his old baggage needed to be dumped.

He hesitated before continuing through the doorway. That wasn't it at all. The truth nettled him. It had nothing to do with need, and good intentions weren't a factor. His heart attested to that every day. Getting involved with a woman left him uncertain what direction he "could" go. Though questions still battered his mind, answers might ease his confusion and strengthen his confidence.

He saved lives for a living. Why couldn't he save his own?

Paula watched the last couple arrive, one she didn't know but remembered from the wedding.

"I think you all know Sal and his wife, Maureen." Devon gazed around the room and stopped at her. "Paula, do remember them? Sal is one of our crew."

She hated being the focus of everyone's attention, especially Clint's. He'd sat nearby, but they'd only talked a short time before Neely and Jon arrived and Clint shifted to his seat. "From the wedding, I think." She sent them a smile, hoping it looked sincere. As happened too often at these events, she'd slipped into her distant mode. Groups made her uneasy, but then she'd rarely been involved in social situations. Her life had been mainly one-on-one.

After they were settled and had poured something to drink, Devon introduced the game. Most everyone knew it except Clint and her, so everyone had to go through the rules while she and Clint tried to understand the game.

Ashley stepped into the living room through the dining room archway. "We play in couples." She grinned at the group. "Sal and Maureen, Neely and Jonny." She paused, her eyes shifting from Clint to her. "Paula and Clint and Devon and me." She pointed to the dining room. "Sit across from your partner."

Paula rose and had started toward the doorway when Sal clasped her arm. "So what's the secret here?" She realized he'd also nabbed Clint with the other hand. "Man, you got this beautiful woman and never said a thing at work." He dropped his hand and guffawed. "Some men are too possessive." He gave Paula a wink and followed his wife into the dining room.

The last two left behind, Clint looked at her and shrugged. "Sorry. He made an assumption, and I hated to—"

"Don't worry about it." Her heart lodged in her throat. "We can't disappoint the man." She managed to grin, relieved her response hadn't sounded as choked as it felt.

Clint slipped his hand around her arm and led her to an empty place at the table. He pulled out her chair and then sat across from her at the folding table.

The game began, and she caught on, as did Clint. Each time they placed their tokens on the correct symbols of the board she wanted to chuckle. Though new to the game, they formed the first sequence at their table. Two completed sequences meant they would win the game.

A few minutes later, Clint laid his token on the board, forming their second sequence. "Sequence."

Paula couldn't help but laugh. "That's two games out of three."

Ashley stood above them shaking her head. "Are you two mind readers?"

Clint's eyes latched to hers. "We've noticed it on occasion."

Heat grew on Paula's face as all eyes focused on her. "The man does have a knack." Though she kept her grin steady, she couldn't help but recall the many times Clint had read her thoughts. The ability wasn't hers as much as his. But the game. Pure luck.

Maureen gave Sal a playful punch. "I wish he had that quality when he goes to the grocery store. I send him for a few items and he comes back with everything but." Her perception added levity and the focus shifted to Sal.

They played the seven games planned, and the last game pumped her spirit. With one sequence completed, she studied the game cards in her hand and knew what she wanted Clint to do.

He hesitated, his eyes raking over his options. Finally he looked at her. "Wish I could read your mind now." He shook his head." I have two choices, and I can't decide which one to play."

Going along with the running joke, she gave him a wink. "I'll concentrate." She gave him a dramatic gaze, and he selected a token and set it down. Her pulse jigged when he placed it on the spot she'd wanted. He looked at her and she could only laugh. Maureen placed her token, and Paula lifted hers and set it on the board. "Sequence." They'd won four of the seven games.

Neely rose, bracing her growing belly beneath her hand. "We have to separate these two next time."

Everyone laughed, and Paula managed to grin along with them, but the reality hit her. Being a couple with someone like Clint would be more than she dreamed. The concept wrapped around her heart, a mixture of longing and disbelief. She'd never felt anything like this before. Neely and Ashley sometimes made reference to God's plan for them. The concept had meant nothing to her, not even a vague understanding, but being a partner with Clint in an activity as simple as a game roused a question. If God had a plan for everyone, was Clint part of her plan or just another disappointment? She spent her life expecting her hopes to be dashed because believing good things would happen created a greater letdown.

The negative thought hit her stomach, but her recent determination chased it away. She'd had enough downers in her life. Maybe, just for once, a new road opening for her could send her on a journey that led to good things.

Sometimes she wished she knew how to pray. She'd ask God to give her a hint of His plan for her.

If He had one. She knew so little about the faith her cousins, even Clint, held so dear. Closing her mind to the possibility wasn't a choice anymore. The seed had been planted and insisted on burrowing deeper. She loved the new walk even though it scared her. But she'd never laughed or smiled so much in her life as she had these past weeks. She wasn't willing to give those up for anything. Especially not misery.

Chapter Four

❦

"Can you handle a spreadsheet?"

Paula's pulse skipped as she studied the manager's stoic expression. "Yes. Which program do you use?"

He hesitated and glanced again at her résumé. "Which have you worked with?"

His evasive response reminded her of the tactic she used. "Excel, Quickbooks, Quantros." She searched for other types she'd heard of. They were all alike...or she hoped they were.

Silence settled around them like a fog. Finally, he closed the file and slid it onto a pile. "We have a few more interviews, and we'll let you know at the end of the week." He rolled back in his chair and rose, his hand thrust toward her. She eyed his navy suit, a bit frayed at the cuff and tight around his paunch. She hoped the worn suit didn't reflect the financial situation of the business.

She stood and grasped his palm, managing a firm

shake though her heart wasn't in it. As with most interviews, she had no idea what they wanted. His vague comments and questions left her puzzled. It all seemed a game. Yet, the truth was with so many people out of work, employers had the advantage. She didn't. "Thank you, Mr.... She glanced at his name engraved on the desk stand. "Mr. Ledworth. I hope to hear from you."

With her bag slung over her shoulder, she turned toward the door and exited, feeling the bite of discouragement. This had been her second interview that day and the seventh since she'd begun looking.

The man had commented on her newness in town and lack of work for the past few months. She'd tried to explain, but his expression let her know he'd heard it before. She massaged her neck as she stepped into the autumn sunlight, and though a slight chill hung in the air, the sun's glare caused her to squint.

A stream of air shot from her lungs when she jerked open her car door. She slid inside and, before she slipped the key into the ignition, she heard the buzz of her cell phone, the first she'd owned since Vic. She glanced at the ID, her anxiety heightening. Classic reality. Hating to get her hopes up, she pressed the answer button. "Paula Reynolds speaking."

She listened, her hope rising. "How much have they offered?" Her heart sank. "That's twenty thousand dollars less than the asking price." Dreams of purchasing Ashley's house dimmed. "Is this normal? I thought we gave them a fair price. More than fair."

Feeling out of her realm, she listened to his explanation. She knew people tried to barter. Why was she surprised? "Okay. So we counter offer."

The more she listened the more disheartened she became. "What do you suggest?" Her stomach sank. She needed every penny, but she also wanted to sell the place.

His voice droned on until she longed to hang up. "No. Not that low. The house is priced to sell already." Though she knew nothing about pricing homes, she plowed ahead. "Offer them five thousand less than the asking price."

She finally gave up. "Okay, counter with half of the difference. Ten. But that's it."

She hung up, her pulse racing. What happened to the concept of the Realtor supporting the client and not the buyer? Jamming the key into the ignition, she revved the motor and backed out of the parking space. Indecisive employers and buyer-pleasing Realtors. Just what she needed.

Once heading back to her uncle's, she calmed. The world spun on a different plane than it had in the past. Change happened, and it wasn't the seller's market or the unemployed with options. If she wanted to work, she needed to hang on. To sell the house, she had to give in.

She longed to talk with Clint. He had a calming

effect on her, but she knew he was working, and her showing up at the fire station wasn't feasible. They weren't even dating. She'd keep her boundaries. Silly, but she established them, and it saddened her. Solidifying their friendship was something she could correct.

Today, she flipped the page. The end was ahead. It could be tragic or happy ever after. She grasped the latter.

Clint finished the floors, one of his tasks for the day. Sometimes he wondered if the crew could get together and hire a cleaning lady. He grinned at his stupid thought, but Paula flashed into his mind as his idea got even more ridiculous. She needed a job and... He'd love to see her daily, giving her support, wisdom, whatever she needed while she made him feel alive again.

The warm feeling curled through his chest. Talk about ridiculous. He'd spent wasted hours convincing himself he was only up for a friendship while half of him had dreams that went deeper.

Devon passed by the doorway, and Devon's words flashed through his mind. *Will you ask her out on a date and not just to talk?* Talk seemed to be their M.O. He settled onto a chair in the day room while questions dropped into his mind. What did he want? Most of the time, he wasn't sure. What did he need? That question was even more vague...except at the moment he wanted to talk with her. She'd been in his thoughts all day.

As quickly as the idea of asking her out, he had another thought. His opinions on finances and savings needed to be stifled. Paula tried to be pleasant, but he recognized irritation building in her, and he'd tried to stop himself from doing more damage than good. Hoping what he said hadn't upset her too much, he decided to move ahead.

He pulled out his cell and hit his contacts. Paula had given him her new cell phone number the day she got it. Curious as always, he asked why she didn't have a cell phone. Everyone did, but she gave one of her evasive responses. He lowered his phone, picturing the day she would open up and let him in.

Startled by the TV's blast, he glanced up to see two of the crew giving attention to the six-o'clock news. Tasks were done for everyone except the kitchen crew. A whiff of something good had sailed past him when he'd neared the kitchen earlier, but his usual appetite had taken a hike. His stomach churned with his indecision over Paula.

Fighting the option to pop the cell phone back into his pocket, he slid his finger along the contact list to the *P*s and hit her number. He waited, his heart in his throat until she answered. But before he could bring up the topic of a date, she had her own priority.

"I was tempted to call you today. I even thought

of driving there to see you. I'm sure you're glad I stopped myself."

An image of her appearing at the station flew into his mind. Bad timing, but he longed to see her.

"But I decided that wouldn't be appropriate. You know me. Sometimes my ideas aren't the greatest until I work them out with a little common sense."

The reference struck him as a spillover from their previous conversation on finances. "You're welcome to drop by. Evenings, though, are best when our scheduled work is finished. Usually after dinner is when families show up. The chief is good about that, unless we—" He closed his mouth, sounding as if he were rattling on and on. "You sound a little upset. What happened?" Dumb question. Why else would she want to see him? He winced. "Or did you hear good news?" He knew better. The tone of her voice signaled a problem.

Silence until she finally spoke. "Sometimes I think I have a loose screw in my head."

"Never. You're just missing a washer." He wanted to cheer her up but he didn't seem to be succeeding. When he noticed two buddies glancing his way, curiosity emblazoned on their faces, he knew he needed privacy.

"Let's get back to my question." To avoid the men's eavesdropping, he wandered out the door into the hallway, searching for an empty room and waiting for her response. He'd already been taunted by some of the guys who Sal had talked with about the

Sequence evening. They all wanted to know about his "secret" girlfriend.

"Yes and no." Paula's voice cut through his thoughts.

He made his way down the hall and found his sleeping quarters were empty. Grateful, he plopped onto his bunk. "Which should I hear first?" He plumped his pillow, braced it against the wall and leaned back.

"I had another job interview today. It wasn't promising, but what really upset me was the call from my Realtor."

That sounded an alarm, and his head popped up for a moment. "Is this the good or the bad?"

"Both."

Though his mind overflowed with possibilities, he was tired of playing mental guessing games. "Tell me the good first."

"I had another offer on the house."

"Okay. That's good. Now what's the bad?" He held his breath, already guessing what she would say. He listened to the details and didn't see the problem. She had an offer but with twenty thousand shaved off the asking price. Not bad. "It could have been worse, Paula."

"Worse? How?"

She'd never sold a house before and her innocence showed. Not wanting to upset her, he started to explain worse counteroffer possibilities. But before he finished, he heard the call for dinner. "Let's do this. Think about it. Tomorrow I'll be home for a couple of days. We'll have time to really talk without listening ears."

A puff of breath whisked through the receiver. "You're in close quarters. I forgot."

She sounded discouraged, and he had so much more to say. "I'll catch a nap in the morning if I need it and give you a call in the afternoon. We can get together then. Will that work?"

"Sure, but I'm sorry I laid this on you, Clint. You have your job on your mind and I—"

"I'm happy to listen and if I can help, so much the better." He chuckled into the phone, hoping she imagined his grin. "And the only thing I have on my mind at the moment is dinner."

"Ah." Tension had eased from her tone. "I should have known. Thanks for listening."

"I'll do more than that tomorrow. See you then, and we can mull over the situation."

"Thanks. See you tomorrow."

He heard the disconnect and stared at the silent phone. "So much for a real date." He slipped it into his pocket and headed to the dining room.

Paula's scowl eased as she finished her story again, this time adding all the details. She eyed Clint, unable to read his thoughts, though she wished she could. Somehow he always read hers— validated at the Sequence party—and though it flattered her in a way, often she disliked his knowing what was on her mind. Waiting to give him time to respond, she worked at patience—something she didn't have. "What are you thinking?"

His gaze had drifted out the window or somewhere else, along with his mind, and she concluded he hadn't heard her. "What are—"

"I don't know what to think. I don't know anything about the house, so if it's a fair price or not, I don't have any way to know. Counteroffers are part of the sale. It's a kind of bartering. You're not the only seller who deals with it, and you have the—"

"I realize the Realtor is involved, but…" Being alone was part of her life, but Clint didn't have any concept of her kind of solitude. His experience even at work was having his crew, his pals. "But I—" Words still failed her. She'd never had anyone offer good advice, not her mother, her few friends or Vic. Especially him. He wouldn't know good advice if it bit him.

"But the final decision is yours." He stared at her a moment. "I'm sure you might feel alone. The Realtor is hired. He wants a sale no matter what. That's how he earns his money."

She nodded, recognizing he understood more than she thought. "That's it. But I've never sold a house. I've never even owned one."

He nodded, his eyes downward, as gears seemed to turn in his head. She recognized his way of analyzing a problem. When his head lifted, a new light shone in his eyes. "Here's the plan. I'm off today and tomorrow. It's already afternoon now so let's take a ride to Roscommon tomorrow morning. I'll look at the house and can make a better judgment. Advice is better based on fact."

Her spirit brightened. "Would you do that? Don't you have things to do at home?"

Clint gave her a wink. "The dust will still be there the next time I have a day off. Ever notice that?"

She laughed despite her heavy thoughts. Clint could do that for her. "I have a collection of dust bunnies that I've grown to love."

He leaned forward, his expression more serious. "I'm anxious to see the house anyway, so it will be a fun trip."

Fun. She wasn't sure. Whenever she entered the two-story farmhouse, her emptiness deepened, thinking of all she'd missed in life that others talked about—affectionate parents, lessons in faith, security without question. The list could go on, but blaming her mother or father had become pointless. So many of her dumb decisions had been her own, and she could only blame herself. The time had come to welcome the present. Wise decisions were long overdue. "You're sure you don't mind?"

"I am or I wouldn't have suggested it. How long to get there? Three hours?"

"A little less."

He gave her an agreeable nod, while a look in his eyes left her longing for a secure life with him. She relaxed against the cushion. "I'm glad you'll have a chance to see it, and I can take a few notes on what to keep if anything and what to give away. I'm not sure that will be fun." She managed a grin. "You mentioned fun."

"Ah, but you don't know the second part of my plan."

She held her breath. "And what does that mean?" Then she remembered the gift certificate they'd won at the game night. He'd never told her what it was for.

"We'll be very close to Frankenmuth on I-75 freeway. Do you like German food?"

She shrugged. "I've never eaten it that I know of, and I've never been to Frankenmuth. Can you believe?"

"No." His brows arched upward. "I thought everyone who lives in Michigan has been there."

The list of things she'd never done got longer.

"It'll turn you into a child again." He rose and sat on the arm of her chair. "Wait until you see."

A child again? "Okay. I believe you."

"And you should." His head lowered a moment, his uneasiness noticeable. "You know the trip to Frankenmuth will be our—" He inched upward, his eyes searching hers. "Our first real date."

First date? Her pulse skittered. "It'll be fun. Thanks." She heard her voice but didn't recall speaking.

His eyes brightened as a look of relief swept

across his face. He grasped her hand and kissed her palm. "It will be. I can't wait."

Warmth seeped along her arm to her chest, leaving a sweet and tender longing.

Clint stood on the gravel driveway and eyed the house. He hadn't pictured the rustic setting. For some reason, he'd imagined a bungalow matching others on the street of one house after the other. He'd been wrong. The white siding stretched across the front with three sets of double windows flanking the front door. A series of wooden steps rose to the long wooden-railed porch with six posts bracing the blue-shingled roof covered with dried foliage from the surrounding pine trees.

His attention was drawn to a white-and-blue garage set back from the residence, where a concrete driveway reached the front of the house and connected with a gravel driveway. Why hadn't they poured concrete all the way to the street? That was a negative for buyers. Scrawny shrubs dotted the beds along the porch and nothing else added color or life to the building. Maybe flowers had bloomed in summer, but he saw no evidence. Loving care could turn the house into a home, but it would take a buyer who wanted to put in some elbow grease.

"What do you think?"

Paula's voice punctured his thoughts, and he turned his attention to her. "I see promise."

A scowl wrinkled her brow. "In what way?"

He'd disappointed her and wished he'd phrased it differently. More positive. "Let's look inside first. I can't make a good evaluation this way." Paula needed encouragement, not doom and gloom. She created enough of that for herself. Maybe today he could learn why.

He followed her up the steps, gazing at the roomy porch while she unlocked the door. When they stepped inside, he gaped at the appealing open staircase, cherrywood, he guessed, rising to the second floor. His eyes swept the room, a solid stone fireplace with a cherrywood mantel and a marble hearth, flanked by two narrow windows. The far end of the room served as a dining area with broader windows giving a view of another porch, but this one seeming to be enclosed with a solid glass wall looking into the woods beyond.

A sliding door led outside and a larger one opened onto the porch. He clicked the lock and strode to view the backyard woods, a blend of pines and deciduous trees, some leafless and others bearing a palette of orange and gold in a surrounding of scrub brush. He tried to imagine the setting in other seasons filled with life and color. The seasonal deck, probably best in the three warmest seasons, held easy chairs, a table that would make a great spot for a meal or playing games. A small TV sat in front of two easy chairs, and a long planter, now holding dead plants, would have added charm to the already inviting space. Today a chill hung on the air and he suspected winter meant closing the door until spring.

He turned and nearly tripped over Paula. She lost her balance, and he grabbed her and drew her close, feeling the softness of her body against his. "Sorry." He managed a smile, hoping to hide the discomfort he felt from his raging pulse. He righted her, then forced himself to step back. "This is nice, Paula. I'm sure families would enjoy a home like this, and it's a great place for children who like the out-of-doors."

Her concern seemed to fade. "I guess it'll have an appeal to some buyers. I'm glad you like it." For the first time since they'd arrived, she appeared to be looking at the room with different eyes. "The place holds too many difficult times for me, and I probably miss the charm." Her expression softened. "I knew my view was skewed, so I listened to the Realtor. He sees lots of houses in this area so I took his advice on the price."

Clint wandered back inside and followed her into the kitchen, a room lacking the counter space and storage many cooks required. "Here's a negative." He gestured to the small size. "Not a lot of room here, but it'll work for some who just cook. Those who like to create may find it lacking."

She shrugged one shoulder. "I wouldn't know about that. Apartments aren't known for their gourmet kitchens."

His spirit buoyed, hearing the lighthearted tone of her voice along with the faint grin brightening her face. He slipped his arm behind her and gave her a squeeze, his chest constricting with her acceptance to his touch.

"I'm sure you'd like to see the bedrooms and baths."

He nodded and followed her. A bedroom and bath, probably the master bedroom, was located in the opposite wing of the house; a window looked out to the side yard and a door opened onto the enclosed porch. One large closet but nothing that would impress buyers and a typical older home bathroom with no convenient counter space or double sink. The shower and tub were combined. Upstairs he found two small bedrooms and a bath in between. He gazed at the bigger one—drab yellow walls with nothing more than a twin bed and dresser.

"This room was mine."

Paula's expression showed her discomfort, and he didn't want to linger. He'd seen enough. He stepped back, then noticed the lone kitchen-style chair sitting near the single window. He could imagine Paula on the chair, her shoulder resting against the windowpane as she wished on a star to get her away from the confines of her life in that house. She'd been right. The bits of charm he'd noted below left much to be desired on the second floor.

When they'd descended the stairs to the living room, she stopped at the bottom. "Well, what do you think?"

"The house has a couple of nice features—the

enclosed porch and this right here." He ambled to the stone fireplace and rubbed his hand along the attractive mantel, feeling dust beneath his fingers. "People who want a rural setting with some charm will find this a good option, but—"

"I know. But someone who doesn't want to live quite this deep in the boonies with a small kitchen and old-fashioned bathroom won't value charm over practicality."

Her jaw tensed, and a faint tic flickered on her cheek. Her eyes were downcast and she didn't move. He feared she might cry. "Something like that."

He opened his arms and approached her, and his heartbeat surged when she stepped into his embrace. She rested her head on his chest, and he moved his palm across the tension in her back, kneading her taut tendons below his fingers.

She breathed a sigh and eased her head upward. "Thanks. I can always count on you to know what I need." She tilted her head back, searching his eyes, and he couldn't stop himself. His lips met hers, a feathery touch he longed to continue, but he eased back.

Her eyes opened, a puzzled look settling on her face, but she stood in place as if she didn't know what she wanted. He opened his mouth to apologize but knew it would be a lie. "I'm glad I came with you today. I think your Realtor was generous with the price. I know dumps are selling for a fortune when they're on lakefront property. Though this one is close to Higgins Lake, it's not on it."

"You're right. Being close enough to walk to a beach was what saved me. In winter, I wanted to scream. It was too cold to go anywhere, and I didn't have a car. Counted on what boys I could find who had one. Not always the greatest experiences."

His head filled with questions, but she'd closed up, so he let them drop. "You're lacking a full driveway, too, and I think that's a downfall."

"It does get muddy in the spring—all seasons, I suppose—except some of the wonderful summer days."

She gestured for him to sit, and he sank onto the worn sofa before she asked her question. "What should I do about the counteroffer?" She slipped into a nearby chair.

"You did the right thing. You halved it. Let's see if they want it badly enough." He ran his hand over the corded upholstery, his finger catching on a loose thread. "They may counter your offer again."

Her downcast eyes edged upward, showing no sign of a smile. "And you think I should accept."

He nodded. "I do if you want to sell."

"You know I do."

Emptiness seeped through him. Watching her face, he knew her mind was filled with unknown concerns and a story that would help him understand, but she didn't trust him enough to share it.

His gut knotted. Would she ever trust him? He pulled himself back. "Paula?"

Her head snapped around to face him. "What?"

"I am curi—" What was the point? She had to be ready. To trust. To unload her burden on someone, and she didn't trust God any more than she trusted him.

Her presence absorbed the air from his lungs until he realized he was holding his breath.

"What's wrong, Clint?" A deeper frown slipped across her face. "And don't tell me nothing."

"I don't understand you. You're bottled up inside, and I'm afraid if you don't pull the cork, you'll blow up. I've tried to give you good advice, haven't I? I listen." He lowered his head, shaking it back and forth. "I don't know what else to do."

"Do noth—" A stream of air shot from her throat. "I don't know what to tell you, Clint. I don't know what you'll think of me or…"

"I'll think you're like I am, Paula. Everyone in this world has problems, things we try to hide. We make horrible mistakes. We don't trust. We doubt ourselves and, even more, we doubt others. We can't imagine that anyone could love us or even care about us." He forced his eyes to meet hers. "But that's not true. It's an illusion we create to avoid opening our hearts and souls. We protect ourselves from vulnerability, and what we do is become even more vulnerable."

Her eyes widened, darting from him to the window and back. She lowered her chin as her eyes closed. "That's true."

He bit his upper lip. In his argument, he'd admitted his own weaknesses. He wanted closure with Elise. Speculation didn't give him contentment. Living life while wondering what he'd done wrong meant not living life at all. He'd bound his life with fear of failing again. Of looking weak. Of being unworthy. Hearing Paula's admission that he was right didn't ease his concern. It made him less confident in himself and even more in their relationship. Whatever it was.

"You know my father wasn't in my life. I barely remember him."

Her voice jerked him upward. "That was difficult, I'm sure." He searched her face, hoping to read her emotion.

She shrugged. "I don't know for sure. I have a vague memory of someone there and gone, but then that was my mother's life, too."

His chest constricted. "She walked out on you?"

"No, but all her men came and went."

All. The word said everything. He managed to keep his mouth from dropping open. He didn't speak for fear of stopping her.

"Mother had no income except government aid. I realized that when I got older. She often dropped me off with one of her friends and wouldn't pick me up for a couple of days. When she finally returned to take me home, a man would be there, his eyes bloodshot—matching my mother's. She'd feed me better food than we usually had and send me to bed. When I woke in the morning, the man was still there. I thought he was my father, but in a few weeks, another man replaced him. When the men were there, my mother had money."

His stomach churned, envisioning the horror of that life for Paula, a child who didn't understand.

"I'd watch them kiss and play around. I always wanted someone to kiss me and hug me the way the men hugged my mother. But my mother never touched me other than to give me a slap for asking a question she didn't like or doing something she thought I shouldn't."

Her face grew dark, and he froze as if his body had turned to ice. Words failed him. No child should endure that life, but there was no point telling her. She'd known even then. A young child who'd witnessed too much. Every response that came to mind rang empty and useless. He'd never experienced a life like that. Though he wasn't naive about bad things happening—he'd witnessed horrible situations in his work—sitting face-to-face with a woman he'd grown to care about killed him.

She stood. "That's enough. Let's leave. This place only makes memories more vivid."

He rose and moved beside her. "Don't you want to take time while we're here to make decisions about what to keep and what to give away?" He rested his hand on her shoulder and kissed her hair, praying he found a way to soothe her struggle.

"I want nothing. Let's go."

He lowered his head and kissed her cheek, longing to hold her and kiss her enough to fill all those lost years. How could he deny he cared more about Paula than any woman in years? Maybe even more than his feelings for Elise.

Chapter Five

Paula carried the dark thoughts into their ride south, but Clint didn't let it last long. He talked about things he did as a child, including visiting Frankenmuth between Thanksgiving and Christmas each year to see the decorated trees in every room of the Bavarian Inn and in the restaurant across the street. His enthusiasm would have captured hers, except she felt guilty knowing she'd avoided telling him the worst part of her story.

But Clint knew how to make her happy, and he'd prepared her with his own childhood stories. As Clint rolled down the driveway to the parking lot of Bronner's Christmas Wonderland, the year-round Christmas store he'd told her about, she couldn't control her squeal. "Clint, you've taken me to the North Pole."

She'd heard about Frankenmuth, but she still couldn't believe the Christmas scenes that lay before her in October. They'd passed a snowman four times taller than the couple who stood beside it, and towering Christmas trees drenched in colorful lights. Where the building faced the highway, the white wall made a backdrop for a nativity scene with larger-than-life figures—angels, shepherds, sheep, donkey and Wise Men huddled around the manager with Joseph and Mary looking down at the baby Jesus.

Her chest tightened, watching little children staring in awe at the giant toy soldiers and gigantic nutcracker characters that lined the paths. Santa and his sleigh delighted even the adults.

"Like it?"

Clint's voice drew her back. "It's amazing. Seeing it is the only way to believe it, but it's true, and if Bronner's Christmas Wonderland looks this amazing in October, I can't imagine what the Christmas season would bring with real snow on the ground."

Slipping his arm around her back, he drew her closer. "I told you it would bring out the child in you."

His gentle voice swept her away. The dark memories faded as he'd promised, and the child in her focused on the colors and novelty of the display and filled her with amazement. "Seeing it did more than make me a child again, Clint." It wasn't really taking her back to childhood at all. That was a place she didn't want to be.

When his gaze caught hers, she read the question in his eyes. "I don't care about the past today. I want to be covered by the happiness I feel here."

He faced her, his arm still holding her close. "I hope all of your days will be filled with the kind of happiness I see in your face right now."

Tears edged her eyes, but they were tears of joy. "I hope you're right."

He leaned closer, his mouth nearing hers, and desire rose for the touch of his lips on hers. Instead, he kissed her cheek and gave her a hug. She managed to smile. "I like your optimism. Can I buy some of that here?" She swept her hand toward the huge building.

"If you could purchase happiness, this would be the place." He lowered his arm and grasped her hand, weaving his fingers between hers. "You'll see."

She followed him through the entrance, and her first view overwhelmed her. Angels rose above her, playing harps and flutes while carolers holding their songbooks rocked to the music they sang. Santas and elves stood in mounds of snow bending their heads and moving their arms at the passersby. She gazed at Clint and shook her head. "I've never seen anything like this."

"Bronner's sells these animated figures to stores and businesses for window displays. It is a wonderland." He pointed ahead. "They have every kind of Christmas decoration or ornament you would ever want."

She followed his lead, her eyes taking in the displays, trees decorated with lights and colorful balls in shades of blue or white with crystal, musical instruments, nutcrackers or patriotic ornaments. Farther ahead she spotted a huge display of the famous Goebel Hummel figurines, each hand painted and each unique, and she wandered the displays of hand-blown balls, wooden ornaments from Germany, wreaths and trees for purchase. Her head spun. She stopped and caught her breath.

Each display captured her interest, and she didn't notice the time until she saw Clint eyeing his watch.

He squeezed her hand. "Ready to go? You're beginning to look dazed."

She chuckled and squeezed back. "Okay, mind reader. Christmas is now embedded in my brain."

"Better than other thoughts using the space."

"You know, you're right. I haven't thought about anything else since we pulled into the parking lot."

"And I'm glad, but my stomach is—"

"Mine, too, and you promised me some German food." She hadn't realized how long it had been since they'd eaten.

The quiet and fresh air wrapped around her as they walked to the car. "You seem to know what it takes to cheer me up."

"Distraction, but it's too far to drive here all the time. I'll have to think of other ways to preoccupy you more often." He grinned, his index finger tapping his cheek. "How about…"

She took advantage of his pause. "How about you being my distraction?" Her pulse skipped as the thought grew and the words slipped out.

He looked surprised but it faded to a wide smile. "That's the best idea I've heard in a long time. I'm happy to do the job, ma'am. I promise to be one big distraction from now on."

She loved his smile. "I hope you keep your promise." He opened the car door and she slipped inside, aware that telling him about her mother had lifted a burden from her shoulders. She'd never told a living soul, and he'd listened without judgment, making her feel less guilty than she'd felt in years.

A short drive and she spotted the inn, white stucco crowned with brown gingerbread siding. As they pulled into the parking lot, she noticed a tower with people gathering below. "What's happening?" She pointed to the crowd.

"I'm the king of distraction. We timed it perfectly." He hurried around to the passenger door, opened it and slipped his hand into hers as he guided her into the gathering crowd. "It's a glockenspiel and it tells the story of the Pied Piper."

As they settled, the tower came to life; doors opened and the story began with carved characters. She zippered her jacket to chase away the chill and watched the Pied Piper lead the children out of town. They never returned. The evil in the story caught her, and visions of the men who came and went in her life turned her stomach.

She spotted Clint's grin as he watched the glockenspiel's mythical story and forced the thoughts
from her mind. Clint brought her sunshine and
flowers even in autumn. His influence helped her
see that life could be beautiful. Now she wished
she'd finished telling him about her messed-up life.
He needed to know the full story. Maybe not now.

When the glockenspiel silenced, the story ended.
Clint wove his fingers between hers and led her
inside. They saw a woman in a traditional dirndl
dress, white puffy short sleeves with embroidery
around the square neckline and a navy corset
threaded with colors matching the print skirt covered by a white apron embroidered with the same
flowers. She smiled and led them to one of the dining rooms within the inn filled with German am-
bience.

While perusing the menu, Paula shifted her
eyes to Clint, who seemed unimpressed with the
vast menu of German foods, but the choices overwhelmed her, and she folded the menu closed and
set it on the table. "You can pick something for me.
I have no idea what these dishes are."

His grin spread warmth up her arms. "Let's get
a combination." He pointed to the choice.

She studied the variety of dishes, never having
heard of rouladen and sauerbraten. The only thing
she recognized was their famous fried chicken. That
was one food she enjoyed. He ordered, and within
minutes food appeared on the table, an abundance

of salads and breads, and before she could sample those, the waitress arrived with bread stuffing, potatoes and finally the meats. Her head spinning, she tried samples of each food.

"Disappointed?" Clint's voice cut through her thoughts.

"Not one bit. I wish I had more room to enjoy it, but I'm about filled up to here." She raised her hand above her eyebrows.

"I see another inch there. Don't stop now."

"Do we have time to pick up some of that fruity bread at the bakery? Imagine it as French toast."

"It's stollen bread. We have plenty of time, but could we pay for it?"

It took a moment to understand his silliness. "I suppose we should." She grinned, feeling his light-hearted spirit spread through her. He made it easier to push her should-haves away. For now she'd enjoy his mood. Outside she would tell him the rest of her story.

After coffee and a piece of strudel they shared, Clint paid the bill, reminding her again this was their first real date. He rose and took her hand as she stood. A sense of God she'd never known overtook her, and a lump gathered in her throat, feeling the gentle touch of the strong firefighter who saved lives more often than she could imagine.

Without trying, he'd been saving hers.

A quick trip to the bakery resulted in more than the stollen bread. A jar of preserves and some of their homemade noodles ended up in her bag. Outside, the late afternoon sun sent a rosy glow on Zehnder's Restaurant across the street. With the look of a plantation, the restaurant appeared as busy as the inn. She eyed the glockenspiel tower overhead, quiet now.

Clint slowed to a stop. "Would you like to walk around town or over that way?" He pointed past the parking lot. "It's a covered bridge, all wood. About 240 feet long."

The delicious food lay like a lump in her stomach. She sensed it was time to tell him more. "Let's walk across the bridge."

He slipped his hand in hers, and they followed the sidewalks and paths to the covered bridge. Watching for traffic, they crossed to the pedestrian walkway on the far side. For a busy day, few cars headed across the bridge and in the shadows of the setting sun, they meandered along the wooden planks, their footsteps making a thud on the boards.

He hesitated near the middle and leaned against the railing. "This is the Cass River." He slipped his arm around her back, his body warming her against the cooler air. When she gazed at him, she saw questions in his eyes.

"You're wondering why I'm quiet."

His grin flickered. "Now who's reading whose mind?"

"I sensed it." She drew in a deep breath. "Clint, it's not all the truth about my mother's men friends—"

"You mean it's not true?" His voice rang with surprise. "I'm glad it's not, but why—"

"No. It's true." Though she'd begun her admission, ruining the lovely afternoon wasn't what she'd wanted. "I shouldn't have stopped when I did. There's more to it."

"More?"

The lump in her throat grew, and she swallowed. "One time when I was about ten, one of her men pulled me to him and kissed me. His mouth was wet, disgusting, and he smelled like cigarette smoke and alcohol. At first it turned my stomach. His hand groped along my body, and I was so frightened I could only scream inside."

"Oh, Paula." His voice shook, and his body tensed. "No."

"My mother walked into the room before anything worse happened, and she sent me to the neighbors'. She must have called them, because Mrs. Johnson was at the door when I arrived, as if waiting for me. When my mother called to have her send me home, he was gone. I never saw him again."

Tension eased from his body, but his breath rattled in his throat. "Thank the Lord your mother came home before anything worse happened." He clasped her arms as he faced her. "That wasn't your fault. You can't blame yourself for—"

She pressed her finger against his lips to stop him. "But there's more—"

"No more. You don't have to relive those memories." He drew her into his arms. "No child should endure any of that, Paula. You can't carry the weight of the man's sin...nor your mother's."

He tightened his hold on her and tilted her chin upward. "You worry because I'm a believer and you don't know what I'll think of you, and then you worry I'll hold your past against you." He searched her face. "Here's what I think. You were a child, living in a world that no child should have to face. You were innocent. How can anyone blame you since this has nothing to do with blame? It has to do with the sin of adults who didn't know Jesus. You were even cheated out of having a relationship with the Lord."

He rested his cheek against her hair. "You are pure and innocent. All you need is to know it and believe it."

She shuddered, tears dripping on his hand. "I've spent my life wanting a fairy-tale love. They're not realistic. Life isn't easy, and neither is love."

"Love can be easy, Paula." He drew her chin upward again, his eyes probing hers. "But you have to love the right things—the right people—and we have to be ready to forgive. That's part of love. Loving your enemies is hard, but forgiveness makes it easier. True love is a gift, freely given. Look at God's love for His children." He lowered his head and kissed her forehead. "You and I are His children."

She'd heard people say those things, but she didn't understand how to love that way.

Footsteps sounded on the planks, and she looked in that direction and saw a family, smiles on their faces, heading their way.

Clint shifted and stepped away from the wall. "I suppose we need to move along."

Though filled with questions, she joined him again heading to the far end of the bridge. Today had opened and closed a door she'd kept hidden from everyone. Releasing it, she realized that her great condemnation came from herself, her shame and guilt. But Clint had called her pure and innocent. She wished it were the truth. He hadn't let her finish her story.

"How'd it go?"

Clint shifted away from the kitchen counter to face Devon and wagged his head. He'd never known a man to be so preoccupied with playing cupid. "How did what go?"

Devon's grin grew. "The date." He wiggled his eyebrows. "You went to Frankenmuth, right?"

"Her mother's place first." Devon's questioning look didn't flinch.

"I know, Clint, but then you went—"

"You must have talked to your wife."

"We do talk occasionally." Devon chuckled, and Clint knew he might as well say something his friend wanted to hear.

"Okay, pal. We had a nice time. Food was excellent. She loved Bronner's with all the Christmas displays. We walked across the wooden bridge." He didn't plan to tell him anything about their conversation or the kiss.

"And?"

"And she bought stollen bread to make French toast."

Devon's grin became a guffaw. "Okay, I get it." Giving him a thumbs-up, Devon strutted away, his laughter following him.

Alone again, Clint leaned his back against the counter while his thoughts sailed to the day with Paula. He'd learned so much about her—things that disturbed him. At least knowing the truth, he sensed relief, and each time he saw her he wanted to see her more.

Their visits were inconsistent, and it was partly his fault, he supposed. At times she seemed to tune him out, and he pictured her telling him to hit the road. When those moments occurred, he understood it was her way of handling problems, but the problem was she ran away. That left him wondering if she chased away those who encouraged her to be open.

He'd never challenged her, but he'd tried to suggest methods in dealing with life that could make a difference. Since learning about her mother's male relationships, he couldn't help but wonder how he fit into the picture. Instead of taking chances, he'd begun to tiptoe around her, but one thing she'd said had given him hope. When he'd playfully mentioned he'd find something to distract her, she'd suggested he was enough. But was that true?

He recognized distraction. She'd become his, so they were on the same path. Maybe the time had come to be open about it and to find out where he stood in her life. For him, the answer became easier even with her confession. He wanted to be confident in a deeper relationship. It was what she wished for, was ready for, and it was what he wished for, what he was ready for.

Grasping the large soup pot, he dried it and slid it into the cabinet. Today he faced kitchen duty. Definitely not his favorite. Give him kids' tours every day. He loved it. He dried the last two pots and a skillet, then wiped down the counter and hung the towel to dry.

With the evening meal finished, he had some free time. He pulled out his cell phone and eyed his contacts. Paula's number rolled past, and he paused. He missed her. Facts were facts. Nothing had preoccupied him as she did recently. Her past sat between them, almost poisoning her present. If she could let it go, she could begin to live again.

As the image slogged through his mind, his own emotional garbage heap lingered in his life. He'd allowed something he had no control over to contaminate his present, causing him to doubt himself and his ability to love right. What was loving right?

He thought he had done that, but had he misjudged himself? People thought of him as strong. Even he accepted his strength saving lives and property, so why had he let the weight of Elise's rejection grow?

One day he prayed he could let it all go, the same as he hoped for Paula.

His focus lowered to the cell phone in his hand. What was he delaying the inevitable for? He pressed his finger on the keypad and listened to it ring. When he heard Paula's upbeat voice, a grin sprouted. "What's up? Something good, I hope."

"You can tell from my voice, huh?"

His smile broadened. "I sure can. What happened?"

"Nothing positive but at least hopeful."

The hopeful comment reminded him of the joy she'd expressed in Frankenmuth, and he sensed his prayers had worked. "Lay it on me."

This time she chuckled. "Two things. First, I had a couple more job interviews, and I felt fairly positive with one of them."

"Great news." His spirit sailed heavenward. "What kind of job?"

"Part-time secretary, part-time accounting. I've worked with their software, and the duties sound like the same type of job I had in Roscommon before I had to quit."

"When will you know?"

She drew in a breath. "He said he had two more

interviews already set up, but that would be it. He'd let me know no later than Friday."

He loved hearing her sound positive. Her voice floated across the phone like music. Not wanting to topple her spirit, he ignored the second interview she'd mentioned. It was safer. "And what's the second thing?"

"The first part's not so good. The people didn't accept my offer on the house and didn't counter offer, so that's that."

A twinge of regret filtered through him, and though he had words of wisdom—he always seemed to have those—he let them go rather than put an edge on the situation.

"But..."

That caught his attention.

"He has two more couples looking at it this week, and I've learned my lesson. I want to sell the house, so I really need to consider my response if they counter offer."

Relief replaced regret. "Good thinking. Winter's coming on and that's not a good time to sell, so it's important to sell now, and my hope is they'll see the value of the property as well as the house. It's more than they'd get in the city."

"Right. I'm trying to think upbeat. I blame you for that." Her voice sounded easier than it had.

"I'll willingly take the blame. I was wondering if you enjoyed your French toast." He cringed at the blatant hint.

"No, I saved it. Maybe one day when you're off, you would like—"

The fire alarm reverberated through the building cutting her off. "Paula."

"I hear it. Go do your job. Be safe."

He clicked off and slipped the cell into his pocket as he ran for his gear.

Chapter Six

Paula paced her bedroom, Clint filling her mind as he always did lately. But today was different. Devon had called to say Clint had been taken to the hospital for smoke inhalation. She'd gone numb, fearing the worst, and the lack of additional news from Devon made her increasingly irrational. Two hours had passed. She wanted to know something, and the longer she stared at the phone, the more upset she'd become.

What did she expect? She'd played the "casual" game with Clint since she'd met him, hiding her real feelings as they grew, because she didn't know what she felt or what would happen. Like a seesaw, one day she wanted a relationship, and the next, it seemed impossible. She had too much damage to be little more than a friend. Yet lately she dreamed of more.

When her uncle went for a sandwich, she slipped into her room. Showing her upset in front of him meant being grilled. And lectured. He'd dropped hints more than once that Clint would be the perfect husband for any woman, making a point by giving her the are-you-listening eye. She remembered Clint's wonderful attributes each time she grappled with her feelings.

Being a nomad, hopping from one residence to another had been her life, depending on who influenced her at the time. She knew right from wrong, but she found it necessary to earn their love. She'd learned her error almost too late.

Now facing Clint's accident, the truth settled in. She wanted more than friendship. He'd given her so much, and she'd offered so little. Yet she couldn't let go of the fear that one day he would learn of her past and it would become a weapon to wound her. But as the possibility arose, it hovered only for a moment and then vanished. Most of her life she'd made bad decisions about men. She had no way to measure sincerity, and even then, her own hunger for love blinded her. But with Clint, life had become different. Her judgment had improved, and his integrity won out over any negative thoughts she had.

When Vic had come along, she'd learned a lesson in love. It was not earned. It was given from the heart. Vic's actions proved that for good. When he appeared in her life sitting beside her on a bar stool, she invited him to stay in her apartment. Since he was between jobs, she loaned him money, supported him, thinking that was it—waiting for the ring and the wedding bells as reality fell on her with a thud.

A noise outside made her jump, and she snatched herself from the dark place. No more. She'd lived in that shadow too long. Her cousins and Clint had opened the windows and let in the light. She'd had enough darkness. She'd danced around her feelings for Clint long enough. She needed to tell him how she felt. Open up and be honest. He'd talked about trust and faith. They seemed to go hand in hand.

She recalled hearing how Devon's firefighter job nearly kept Ashley from letting herself fall in love. Though how her cousin could avoid becoming enamored, she had no comprehension. From the day she'd met him, Paula witnessed a tender, loving man who was worth the worry of a possible injury. So far, Ashley said his worst wound had been a sprained ankle. Paula shook her head. That was something even she could handle.

She sank onto the bed, knowing she couldn't hide out in her room forever. She pulled her phone from her nightstand, deciding who to call. Ashley? Devon? The hospital? She didn't know which one.

"Paula?"

A soft tap nudged the door. She froze. "Just a minute." Pulling up her shoulders, she eyed herself in the mirror and worked her face to what she hoped was a casual expression. She would never fool Clint, but maybe she could her uncle.

When she pulled the door open, Fred held the cordless phone toward her. "Thanks. Is it Devon?"

He nodded and strode back into the living room.

She'd forgotten Devon probably didn't have her cell number unless Clint gave it to him for some reason. Holding her breath, she pressed the phone to her ear. "What's the news, Devon?"

"I only have a minute, but I knew you were waiting. They've done an X-ray and see no permanent damage they can identify now. They may do a bronchoscopy if he appears to be struggling to breathe, but he's getting oxygen and they're hopeful. They're keeping him tonight."

Company? She wanted to know if he could have visitors, but she held back her question.

"You might be able to see him later if you'd like."

Had she spoken aloud?

"He's resting now. He's taken meds for a headache, and they said he'll sleep for a while."

"Thanks, Devon. I've been worried." More than worried. "Is he at Beaumont?"

"Right. If I hear any more I'll give you a call. I'm at work so I need to scoot."

She thanked him again and hung up. He sounded exhausted. Fighting a fire, especially a bad one, which this appeared to be, had to take every bit of energy the men had.

Emerging from her room with the phone, she returned to the living room and set it on the cradle, realizing her hand was trembling. "Thanks, Uncle

Fred. Devon said they'll keep him tonight, but he'll be okay as far as they can tell."

He lowered the volume on the TV. "You'll go there."

Question or statement? "He's resting, and—"

"And I'm sure he'd love to open his eyes and see a friendly face." He gave her the baited look she expected.

"Maybe you're right."

"No maybes. The guy's sweet on you, and you're just not seeing it." He gave her one of his coy looks. "Or do you see it?" He guffawed and hit the volume button.

That was Uncle Fred. He loved to make people squirm. She wondered how his girlfriend, Alice, liked it? Although she hadn't heard him mention her in a while. Perhaps she'd had enough. That made her chuckle. *You'll go there.* His statement resounded in her mind. Maybe she would.

Clint lifted his eyelids and squinted. The light from the hallway speared through the curtain, blinding him. His lungs burning, he rolled over and coughed with a sizzling sting as if lighting a match. He fell back against the pillow, trying to pull the pieces of his memory together. The image seared through his brain—an out-of-business auto repair shop, flames, smoke thick as muddy water, a flash and fire surrounding him.

He slid his hands over his arms and shifted his

legs, testing his limbs for injury. Only his lungs burned. His thankful prayer rose heavenward. In that mess, he could have been seriously burned or dead. Had he been careless? Questions overtook him, and he searched for answers as he dug deep to recall the details of what had happened.

When he rolled to his side, another raking cough seared his chest, and in moments, the curtain slid back, and a nurse stepped into the room. "How are you doing? Pain?"

"Just when I cough. It feels like fire."

"You're on medication for the cough, but let's put you back on oxygen. Once you get this cough under control you'll be able to go home. You'd like that, wouldn't you?"

He nodded as she stepped back through the curtain, and as she did, the light from the hallway shone on a figure seated near the drape-covered windows. He focused, and his surprise turned to pleasure. "Paula."

"It's me." Instead of rising, she remained seated.

He beckoned to her and, looking uncertain, she rose hesitatingly. "I'll be in her way." She tilted her head toward the curtain, her long hair disheveled as if she'd jumped out of bed to be there. "She's probably getting the oxygen equipment and will be right back."

He wiggled his finger again. "Just for a minute."

Though hesitant, her slender frame inched closer, her tender, lovely eyes shifting toward the curtain as if waiting for the nurse to appear again." Do you need something?"

A relationship with her was what he needed, but he'd wait on that topic. "What time is it?"

She pointed to the clock on the wall. "Evening. Nine-thirty."

"How long have you been here?"

She lifted her shoulders. "Awhile."

Her evasiveness let him know she'd been sitting there a long time. His heart turned to mush. "Thanks for coming. He saw question in her eyes. "It means a lot to me, Paula."

A grin inched across her face. "I guess some people will do anything for company."

His usual wit eluded him. He tried to pull himself up to be more sociable, but exhaustion sent him down again even after all the sleep.

Before he could ask her to raise the head of his bed, the nurse came through the curtain.

Paula's head jerked toward the sound, and she backed away, catching her foot on his tray table.

She shoved it out of the way and sank into the chair as the nurse entered.

The woman crossed to his bed and inserted a gadget into the wall and then attached tubing. Though he tried to watch what she was doing, his head felt too heavy to hold up so he lay back down.

As if understanding, she walked to the end of the bed and he felt his torso rise. "Are you comfortable now?"

"Thanks. I'm fine." He had stretched the truth, but if anything made him feel fine while being trapped in a hospital bed, Paula's presence did.

His eyes fixed on her quiet form sitting in the most comfortable chair by the window. The nurse worked beside him doing something he didn't care about anymore. Finally, she faced him and attached the nasal cannula into his nose, a prong in each nostril. The sting in his chest remained, but breathing took less effort, and he was grateful for that. She checked the airflow again and gave him a wink as she slipped past the curtain.

He hesitated a minute to make sure she was really gone, then turned his attention to Paula, who had filled his thoughts for weeks. He patted the bedside. "I can't see you way over there."

"Are you sure she won't be right back?" She shifted her eyes to the curtain. "I don't want to be in her way."

"You're not in my way, and I'm the only one here at the moment." Though he knew he looked terrible with the tubing and prongs in his nose, now wasn't the time for pride. Paula beside him was far more important than his ego.

He'd longed to kiss her earlier before any kind of oxygen apparatus was attached, but despite his reservation, he beckoned her again, trusting that if the Lord had plans for Paula and him, who was he to doubt his gut feelings? "Did I lose a day?"

She shrugged. "It's still October fourth." For the

first time since he'd noticed her, a faint grin slipped across her face.

"I'm glad I only lost hours and not days." He beckoned her again. "Pull your chair over here."

She rose and walked to his side. "Can I do something for you?"

He nodded, his pulse quickening as he looked into her eyes.

"What?" She looked at the tray table, then the nightstand.

He gazed at her, hoping his eyes told her what he longed for.

A questioning look wrinkled her forehead, and then she flushed. He assumed she caught his innuendo, seeing his silly expression behind the tubing.

Digging deep for courage, he pointed to his lips, and his finger hit the IV tubing. He chuckled. "Do the best you can?"

Before leaning over, she glanced at the curtain again, still concerned about the nurse's intrusion. Her lips touched his as gentle as a fluttering moth. Her eyes captured his, and she lowered her lips again.

His heart went wild with cartwheels. When he caught his breath, he drew her hand to his and kissed it. "How about pulling that chair closer?"

She glanced behind her, then walked to the window and slid the chair next to the bed.

Each movement pleased him—her easy gait, her nervous glance, her rosy lips. The pressure of her mouth remained on his, and when she sat, he drew her hand into his, weaving his fingers between hers. "You have something on your mind."

Her look acknowledged he was correct. "I know firefighters are brave, but are you really okay?" Her eyes probed his heart.

"What do you think?" He gave her a toying look, hoping their kiss would answer her question. "I'm more than okay now."

A faint flush tinted her cheeks though worry still appeared on her face. "I can't help being concerned." She grazed her index finger over his hand. "I want to know what happened to you today."

He drew back as the burn sizzled in his lungs. He muffled the cough, not wanting to add to her concern. "Didn't you talk with Devon? I thought he'd fill you in on the details."

"Me?" Her eyes widened. "I only knew you were being treated for smoke inhalation. Devon was still at work and had to hurry." She lowered her eyes a moment. "I didn't know a thing and that's why I wanted to come, but I didn't think it was appropriate for me to be here."

"Inappropriate?" He tried to cover his scowl.

She pressed her lips together. "To be honest, Uncle Fred was the one who insisted I visit you."

He pictured Fred with his playful manipulation. "He's a good man."

An uneasy smile sneaked to her face. "Well, I'm not your...you know...." She paused, as if wishing she'd not said what she did. "After my uncle's harassment, I decided I'd better get here and find out what happened."

"I'm glad you minded him. Otherwise I'd be lying here alone."

"None of the crew came to see you?"

"They're still on duty. The chief called to make sure I'm okay. A few may stop by tomorrow when they're off." He shook his head. "Really, I'll be fine. No permanent damage."

"I hope." She gave his fingers a squeeze. "But you still haven't told me what happened."

Though reassured that she did care about him, he'd already worked through the experience without much success. The memory of the day lay like a lump in his mind as he struggled to make sense of it all. "The building was some kind of empty car repair place or a warehouse. It was full of grease and oil, grunge all over the floors. Flammable. We knew it was combustible, because the smoke was thick and black."

"And then what happened?"

"I got into my SCBA and regulated the air before—"

"What's an SCBA?"

"Self-contained breathing apparatus. It's a device we wear to avoid smoke inhalation, especially smoke like that, so thick. Like mud."

She nodded, her eyes still flashing concern.

The dusky images became clearer. "I couldn't

remember much when I first woke, but I'm recalling more now. I think I was trying to locate the source of the fire—it was basically an empty building—and we—"

"Were you the only one who went inside?"

"No, but I was ahead of them. Some were dragging out hoses while we assessed the situation." He wished he could answer more clearly. "The next thing I remember was the roof crashing around me. Praise God, it missed me, but it blocked me in. No escape except through fire. The next thing I know my SCBA isn't working like it should. I felt as if I couldn't breathe, and I had to pull it off."

"Why?"

He studied her then realized what she meant. "It's rare that something goes wrong with the apparatus. We check our gear every morning. I didn't find a problem. I'm sure they'll go over it and find out what went wrong."

"So you were breathing that horrible smoke."

His pulse lurched as the recollection overwhelmed him. It was that or suffocate. He lifted his shoulders, feeling the need for more air. "Thank the Lord, the guys pulled me out. I don't know how. The fire was spreading...." He drew in a breath to conquer his emotions. "And I would have been gone." He squeezed her hand, wishing he could promise it wouldn't happen again. It was a part of his job to save lives in dire situations, and he'd joined the other men knowing that.

She rested her cheek on the bed railing. "I want you to feel better and get home." She glanced at the clock. "Tomorrow?"

"I hope." Worry etched her face. He drew a deep breath, and fire raked through his lungs again. He struggled to hold back his cough.

She rose while an unreadable expression washed across her face. "I'm going to let you rest. I'll call you tomorrow or—"

"I have my cell phone. I can call you when I learn something." He hated to see her go, especially since her mood had changed so rapidly.

She leaned over the railing and brushed her hand across his hair. "I hope you rest well tonight."

His lips ached to have her kiss him again, but she drew back, stood a moment and, with a wave, slipped around the curtain.

He listened until her footsteps faded. Loneliness enveloped him. Paula had impacted him in a way that was hard to explain. She'd captured him for many reasons. The most touching part was her vulnerability. He didn't need to be a psych major to recognize that. He hadn't escaped being susceptible, either, but he'd succeeded in hiding it better than Paula. Even now, he felt it. Though he'd lived alone for a long time, as she walked away tonight, he felt empty without her.

Paula had lain awake half the night, sorting through her feelings. No matter what she did, she couldn't dismiss the truth. Clint made life worth living. She hadn't felt so much a part of anyone's life in years, not even her cousins and Uncle Fred, who'd saved her in their own way.

She pulled the stollen bread and a package of link sausage from the freezer and, though she suspected Clint had eggs at his house, she didn't want to take a chance. Just in case, she wrapped four eggs in paper towel and found a small container they fit inside safely, she hoped. Though nervous about her visit, when she heard he'd be home by late morning, she'd promised him breakfast, and he'd readily agreed. She piled her wares into a grocery bag, tossed her purse over her shoulder and headed outside.

A chilly breeze ruffled her hair and the scent of moldering leaves and grass filled her senses. Flower beds looked empty except for some mums and remnants of a few brave petunias. She loved spring, when tulips and hyacinth gave way to purple coneflowers and daisies and the air filled with the sweet fragrance of roses and lavender. Yet even in autumn, nature had put a stamp of approval on the changes in her life. Like autumn, the old was dying and the new was waiting for spring to return, both outside her and inside.

She unlocked her car, rested the food bag on the front seat and latched the seat belt around it. Smiling at her passenger, she backed out of the driveway and made her way into traffic, her excitement rising as she neared Clint's house.

A positive feeling comforted her. She wanted to get things out in the open. Clint's asking for a kiss, his continual tenderness meant something. How could she doubt his feelings? And yet, she'd been duped before. Not just Vic, but a few others along the way. She'd been gullible. The fear of it happening again stole her confidence. She questioned her common sense at every turn.

Clint's lovely home came into view; a few roses still clung to the thorny limbs and the broad leaves of hosta, some in dark green, others variegated in whites and greens, hadn't given up yet. The landscape looked fresh and neat. Clint worked hard on his days off to make his property look attractive, but the attractiveness didn't end there.

She'd grown to love his slightly salt-and-pepper hair, a contrast to his youthful features. The look added confidence and balance to his demeanor. He had a solid head on his shoulders. She'd become aware of his concern for her security and financial situation, and after noticing her irritation, he now tried to hide it. He'd failed, but she couldn't fault him for that. His morning call had lifted her spirits, and now she had one piece of good news for him, which lightened her worries though she knew better than to count on it until she was positive.

She unlatched the grocery bag from the seat belt and headed inside.

Clint met her at the door with a hug. "You kept your promise. I like that."

"You like it most when it has to do with food." She cast him a smile as she flashed past and headed for the kitchen. His raspy voice hadn't improved. She heard it now and earlier on the phone, and she couldn't help but worry.

His footsteps scuffed behind her. "What's in the bag?"

She flashed him another grin. "Think back. I'm sure you'll remember."

His smile broadened. "French toast with a German influence, I hope."

"Correct on both counts." She spread the ingredients on the island. "I need a bowl, a cutting board and bread knife, and a fry pan with about a half-inch of cooking oil."

He moved away, pulling out what she'd requested while she went to work on their breakfast.

When Clint had done as she asked, he hovered beside her, and though she loved his nearness, she knew he should be resting. Besides, she'd probably do something stupid by her distraction with him so near. Nothing worse than burned food. "You're recuperating. You need to sit." She pointed to the stool on the other side of the island.

He questioned her with a look, but rounded the counter and settled on the seat.

She shifted her attention and beat the eggs. "How long will you have the rasp?"

He shrugged. "For a while, I suppose. X-rays looked good and my membranes were clear. The rasp and breathlessness is common with smoke inhalation. It should improve as I heal. They gave me an inhaler and a scrip for pain meds if I need them. I'll go back in a week. If I have problems before that, I'll call them."

She liked his answer, and his course of action made sense to her. "I should stop worrying, I suppose."

"Good idea. Don't worry, but you can still care about me. I like that."

"I do care. I think you know that, and I know you're concerned about me, too, so I have some good news...I hope."

His eyes widened "Job?"

"No." She shrugged and let it drop. Worrying about something she had no control over was a downer, and she loved the good feelings she had today. "About the house."

He drew back, his dark eyebrows lifted as if anticipating what she had to say. "Is it—"

"Almost, I think. I countered the offer, and they countered back." She eyed him to hear his response.

"And?"

"I accepted, and now I wait for the loan approval."

He jumped from the stool, a cough interrupting his eager "Wahoo!" He blocked the cough with his hands and rounded the island, drawing her into his embrace. She let the fork sink into the bowl as she hugged him back, loving the feel of his arms holding her close. Clint's presence gave her hope. She felt protected and cherished, a wonderful new feeling.

He drew her closer and gave her a squeeze. "I'll pray that it happens, Paula."

Prayer. Once again her lack of faith undid her confidence, but she thanked him since prayer meant much to him. She drew back, hoping her voice sounded lighthearted. "I need two hands if you want to eat."

"What do you think?" With a wink, his arms slipped to his side, but he didn't move. He dragged in a breath and returned to the stool, where he folded his hands on the countertop.

Seeing his playfulness heightened, she longed to clear the things that troubled her. If she told him all of her past, it might make everything different between them, She could let him know how she felt without fear. Yet it was too chancy. She couldn't act on anything until she knew he could accept her as she was. A man of faith would never form a relationship with a nonbeliever. That was one strike against her. And if he knew everything about the life she'd led, it would be two strikes against her. She knew what a third strike could mean. Pulling her mind back from her darkened thoughts, she dipped the last thick slice of stollen bread into the egg mixture and placed it in the fry pan. The soft sizzle warned her to lower the temperature, and she waited a moment before flipping them.

She enjoyed seeing the bread's soft brown color

along with its crisp texture almost as much as she enjoyed watching Clint pull plates from the cabinet and hit the button on the coffeemaker. It gave her a sense of family. Her family.

"Could you put those sausages in the microwave? About a minute."

He set the sausage on a plate covered with paper towel while she turned the second batch of stollen over to crisp the other side. A moment later, a gurgling noise of the coffee seeping into the pot sent up a tantalizing scent of rich Kona coffee, Clint's favorite.

He added silverware to the table, and without her asking, he produced a bottle of maple syrup as the buzzer sounded on the microwave. He checked the sausages and hit the thirty-second button.

In moments, she added a plate of the French toast to the table and slipped into a chair as Clint set down the sausages. He poured the coffee and joined her, folding his hands and lowering his head.

His action caught her unexpected, though it shouldn't have, and she was thankful she hadn't taken a drink of coffee or speared a piece of French toast. She bowed her head, her hands in her lap, and though uneasy with her lack of faith, she respected his.

Clint's prayer, though short, pronounced his thankfulness for his rescue from the fire, the meal she'd prepared and for her company. The sincerity of his words spread through her chest. She wished she could count on someone powerful like God to lean on. Though Clint's strength and wisdom had become her stronghold, since yesterday she'd faced his vulnerability.

When she raised her head, Clint's focus was on her, and she realized he'd been watching her. Instead of explaining, she motioned toward the food spread before them. "Help yourself."

He took a minute to react, and then forked two pieces of French toast and a couple of sausages onto his plate. After he slathered on the maple syrup, she watched him take his first bite of the stollen. Pleasure brightened his face.

He pointed to the dish with his fork. "This is excellent French toast, Paula. I've never had anything like it. French toast will be nothing without your special touch."

"It's not me. It's the bread." She lowered her eyes and tasted the dish, agreeing to herself it was excellent.

They ate in silence except for an occasional request for more syrup or a coffee refill, and in the quiet, she reveled in her surprise that he was even here with her, but more, she longed to understand their relationship.

She had no idea how she would broach the subject, but she would when they finished.

Chapter Seven

Clint insisted upon clearing away the dishes. Rest was one thing but getting better meant rebuilding his stamina. He didn't want to be away from his job longer than necessary. While he loaded the dishwasher, Paula sat at the island wrapped in thought. He observed her quiet struggle, longing to help her resolve whatever bothered her.

Her look concerned him on one hand, but on the other, earlier she'd been as bright as a summer sun. Paula had shown her emotional pendulum more than once, buoyant with lightheartedness and then as dark as a coming storm. He wished he could change it, but liking someone and wanting to change them never worked. For better or worse fit not only wedding vows but also friendship.

For years the thought of wedding vows had dissolved in mist, but more and more, the idea entered his mind, the desire to find a soul mate, to bear children, to raise them in love and faith. To become a family. What could be better than that? Sometimes he suspected Paula longed for the same. Other times, not so much.

Paula's darkness concerned him. It was something buried deep, an open wound, a knife still piercing her heart. A lost love? An unanswered dream? An unforgivable sin? What could a tender, caring, vulnerable person have done that was so unforgivable?

"Five dollars for your thoughts?"

Paula's question split through his musing. He hesitated, not knowing what to say. "Five? That's a good price." Evasiveness never worked with Paula, but this time he hoped so.

"Inflation." She rose and came to his side, leaning against the counter. "But I'm asking the question you always ask me. What's on your mind?"

As he feared, his ploy had failed, while the truth sat like a pile of rocks in his gut. "Nothing important." He'd told her a lie, and looking at her expression, she hadn't believed him. "That's not so. I'm thinking about you. It's something I do a lot."

She nodded. "And I think of you…a lot."

He closed the dishwasher door and drew her into his arms. "I think we need—"

"Me, too."

Her immediate comprehension and response dispelled the rocks in his stomach. But he knew Paula's input to a discussion was often more like words balanced on a fence, ready to fall into impenetrable silence. Though he longed to hold her closer and press his lips against hers, he controlled the desire, sensing finally the time had come to take a big step forward.

He guided her by the hand into the living room, where she settled on the sofa. He shifted a nearby easy chair to face her. She looked as edgy as he felt. Though she'd responded without hesitation, he couldn't guess if her reply was one he wanted to hear or one he wished he'd not requested.

"Should I begin?" He studied her while she mulled over his question.

Finally she broke the silence. "Let me ask you about something first, okay?"

Concern prickled down his spin. "It's fine with me."

She stared at the floor, her cheek ticking with tension while his apprehension grew.

"Though we have some great things in common, Clint—" her head lifted and her eyes captured his "—we have one big difference."

Hope shriveled in his belly, and he longed to divert the conversation with humor, but his idea fizzled in the light of her serious expression. "I'm sure we do, but is it really a major—"

"This one is."

He sat stunned by her quick response. His mind shuffled through a multitude of possibilities, and then it hit him. "I'm a Christian."

She closed her eyes, a faint nod the only movement she made. "That's major. Your faith is built-in. It's not an addition."

He rose and drew her up with him. "It's built-in. That's true."

"I think so much of you, Clint. I think your faith is part of what I admire. You have something to lean on when times get tough even if it's what some call…a crutch." She tilted her head back, her eyes searching his. "I wish I had a crutch like that."

Faith wasn't a crutch, as she called it, but he understood that many people without faith saw it as such. It was something so deeply seated in the heart that taking it away took life away. It depleted who he was and always would be—a child of God. And more important, a forgiven child of God. "I wish I could give you the assurance of God's strength, his forgiveness, which is something we all need."

She flinched at his reference to forgiveness, and it validated his earlier attempt to discover for certain what deep wound she hid. Forgiveness, but for what? Asking would defeat their step into the open. She needed to tell her story of her own free will. A lamp lit in his mind. "Paula, did you know that one of God's gifts to us is free will? We have the right to make choices."

A scowl inched across her face. "What about bad choices?"

"It's what we do as part of the human race. We make good ones and bad. We bungle and we pick ourselves up and move—"

"But how do you do that, Clint? How can you pull yourself from a manure pile and come out smelling like flowers? You carry the stench with you."

"Part of God's gift is removing the stink. If we are sorry for the sin, if we atone, He washes us clean. Clean from our stupid mistakes and clean from our blatant sins." While she mulled his words, he shifted toward the sofa and encouraged her to sit. When she did, he settled beside her.

"Why?"

Praying for wisdom, he answered. "Because He's our loving father, and we're His children. When children stumble and fall, parents pick them up and bandage their wounds. When a child lies or steals, even though he knows it's wrong, the parent doesn't stop loving him. They don't love his behavior, but they love the child. So they guide him in a way that corrects the error, and if he's really sorry, they stand by him with their forgiveness."

Deep creases lined her forehead, and he remained silent. Paula had to work this through on her own. He couldn't hand her faith. He could only offer answers.

"I understand what you've said." She shrugged. "But I didn't have a father, and my mother wasn't really involved in my life. I saw this reflected in some of my friends' families and here in Ferndale. Uncle Fred taunts his girls with his playful ways, but he stands by them. His love is always evident."

"That's the key. Love. Jesus said, there's faith,

hope and love but the greatest of these is love. Love opens us to every attribute we can have—faithfulness, kindness, compassion—everything that God asks us to be." He wove his fingers with hers, his mind grasping for words that God might give him. "You have those qualities, Paula. You're filled with love. I see it with your family. I see it in the way you adore the children. And you have the greatest—love."

Tears edged along her lashes, but she let them be. "Then what happened to my faith and hope? Tell me where they are."

His chest tightened. *Help me, Lord.* "You have the seeds."

"Seeds?" Her scowl deepened. "I don't get it."

Tension knotted his shoulders. "A farmer sows seeds. If rain doesn't come, he waters them and welcomes sunlight, and they grow. But...if the farmer plants seeds, and a merciless sun beats on them with no rain, and he neglects to water them, they die."

She seemed to weigh his words. "I understand with seeds in the earth, but in me?"

"With love, you have the seeds of faith and hope planted inside you, God-given, but you have to water them and give them light."

Her eyelids lowered and her mental struggle showed on her face.

"The light and rain are God's Word, fellowship with others who can strengthen your walk, and one day, baptism. But it can't be done by others, Paula.

It's your desire to open your heart to God, and the Holy Spirit will help you do the work." His words rang in his head. "I'm not a preacher. I'm just a person bungling my walk through life, trying to do what God wants me to do."

"What if we're not worthy?" Her eyes seared his, emphasizing the depth of her wounds.

"All God's children are worthy. That's not even a question. If you had ten children, would you see any of them more worthy than the others?"

She sat a moment and then shook her head. "I guess not."

"That's your answer."

"I need to ponder this, Clint. Something inside me wants to understand. I see faith in you and Uncle Fred, Neely and Ashley—especially her. I'm sure her faith got her through the loss of her husband and the strength to move forward in life. I want that kind of faith."

His chest inflated until he feared it would burst. "That's all you need. Wanting opens the door."

Tension left her shoulders, and she sank against the sofa cushion. "That's all?"

"Learn by using the opportunities around you. One day the light will shine."

"I hope so." She shifted onto her hip and faced him. "Thank you for your patience."

Her sincerity touched him.

"And now it's your turn."

His turn? He parted the heavy thoughts in his mind, searching for her meaning.

"You asked me if you should begin."

The faint curve of her lips carried him back. "Right. That seems hours ago." He dipped into his thoughts until he remembered where he wanted to start. "Okay, here goes. I guess you've been worried that your lack of faith would stop me from having feelings for you."

She nodded. "I sense you care, but I've carried a bug outside rather than kill it. That doesn't mean I want it as a pet."

Her example lightened the moment, and a chuckle escaped him. "You're far more than a bug to me, Paula. I'm enamored by you. You should know that."

"I hoped, but then I've made misjudgments before."

Her statement jarred him as if she'd elbowed his ribs. Was that it? Had she made such horrific mistakes it tainted her perception? The awareness caused him to rethink his approach. "But we learn from mistakes. Sometimes it takes a while, but I think in time we feel a bond growing, a bond without questions. We can't change people. You get what you see if you really look. We're not only our words but also our actions. When our words and our actions clash, that's a warning sign. I hope you haven't seen any discrepancies in me."

"I haven't, but even that makes me question if I'm just blind to them."

He slipped his arm around her shoulders and drew her closer. "You're not blind. I'm pretty much out in the open."

She remained silent for a while, her head on his shoulder, and he held her.

"You are when I think about it. Yesterday I saw one thing about you I'd never seen." She tilted her head upward, her eyes drawing him in. "You're vulnerable, just as I am."

"I am. We all are even when I try to be a macho man." He took a deep breath. "So here's my problem, and it's one way we're the same. I've had a hard time getting over Elise's flight from the altar and from me. She waited right to the end. Not exactly a runaway bride but almost. We had the hall, the ring, the church—everything but the invitations."

Her expression softened. "That hurt."

"It almost destroyed me. I'm a firefighter. A brave hero in children's eyes, but I realized that day that I was weak and, as you said, vulnerable. I hated the feeling. I almost hated myself. I wanted to know what I had done, how I could have fixed it and made Elise happy. How—"

"Did you ever think you couldn't make her happy?"

She startled him. "Maybe that's the issue. What am I lacking that I—"

Paula pressed her finger on his lips to silence him, then slid her palm to his cheek. "That's not it at all. Happiness is inside us. I'm a prime example of someone who's taken a long time to face that. There are people in the world whose happiness is to be unhappy. They're never content. They jump from one thing to another searching for happiness, but each time they move, they take with them what it is that makes them unhappy."

"They make themselves unhappy. Is that what you mean?"

She released a ragged breath. "Right." She lowered her head. "I'm going to be honest with you, Clint. You're the first person I've said this to, and it's something I've just begun to learn. I wanted to be loved so badly that I threw myself into everything that I thought would give me love. I failed every step of the way. Recently I realized that never having felt love, I didn't know what it is. I didn't love myself. I felt unworthy. Hopeless. Useless. Name it—anything negative—and that was my identity."

He swung his head from side to side as words failed him. He drew her deeper into his arms and sought her lips, letting every feeling he'd had for her flow freely. He'd been scared. She'd lacked hope and self-esteem. They were two muddled people who needed each other. He sensed it more than he'd sensed anything.

Her mouth clung to his, her body shaking in his embrace. Tears ran along his cheek and he wasn't sure if they were hers or his own. And he didn't care.

When he eased back, he nestled her to his side.

No words were needed. They had made a big step, and their relationship didn't need to be defined. It needed to grow with confidence and with love if God blessed it.

He prayed the Lord would.

Paula sat across from the buyers, signing the papers to finalize the sale of her mother's home. Her check lay on the table between the Realtor and mortgage lender rep, whose name she had missed in her nervousness. Though signing her name should have been a relief, somewhere inside her it left her nostalgic, even sad.

Not wanting to sink into the old despondency, she focused on the buyers as they signed the papers, and she accepted the check for the house. Their offer, even though it hadn't been as generous as she'd countered, no longer mattered. They were thrilled with the house, and the check in her hand moved her one step closer to making a new life for herself.

"Miss Reynolds."

The Realtor's voice pulled her from her thoughts.

"You have thirty days to clear your belongs from the property. Anything left behind will become property of the new owners."

Although she didn't want anything from the house, she didn't want to leave a mess for the couple who bought it. "I'll see it's taken care of."

"Thanks." Ron Downs, the new owner, smiled and extended his hand. "We appreciate it."

She acknowledged his thanks and slipped the check into her purse.

The Realtor rose, shaking hands with her and the couple, and when she'd been as social as she needed to be, she slipped through the door and headed for her car.

Today wasn't a day she wanted to plow through the house deciding what to do with the furnishings inside. The check lifted her spirit, and returning to her uncle's made sense. She could talk to him about who to contact to empty the house.

As she backed out of the parking place, her cell phone beeped, and she stopped and checked the ID. Her heart tumbled when she saw the caller's name. She hadn't expected this call after the long wait. But once she heard the employer's voice, she readied herself for the news. "Sorry about the delayed call. I had a family emergency that took a couple of days, but I hope you're still available. We've decided that your qualifications are perfect, and I want to offer you the secretarial/accountant job we discussed."

Her hand shook as the good news registered. "Thank you and, yes, I'm still available. I've been hoping you'd call, so you've made my day."

"We're excited to have you join our staff. I'll need you to come in to fill out the paperwork and that will be it."

"When would you like me to start?" She held her breath, concerned about getting her mother's house emptied.

"Can you begin October fourteenth? That gives you a week."

A week. Her mind whirred. Could she get that mess finished in a week? It didn't matter. The job did. "That's fine. I look forward to joining your company."

Although she still had a long drive home, before she hung up, she made arrangements to take care of the paperwork. That would be one task completed. She would deal with the other issue when her mind cleared.

When she clicked off, she hit her call log and lowered her finger to Clint's number, but stopped herself and dropped the phone in her handbag. Instead, she took a chance he would be home, and she could stop there on her way to her uncle's.

She anticipated her news—her uncle Fred's encouragement and Ashley's thrill that she could now purchase the house, but Clint's potential reaction was a mystery. His concern could still be her finances. What she wanted was hearing his pleasure.

She wiped away the worry. Clint's opinions were his own. She wasn't stupid, and no matter what else, the day she and Clint had talked about their feelings had been a highlight of her happiness. She clung to it, knowing she still had things to confess, but she'd hinted at the worst, and, despite that, he seemed to enjoy her company and being friends. Baring her soul could come later...if one day the relationship grew from friendship to something more.

Something more. An expected longing coursed through her, picturing Clint's arms holding her close, his lips on hers. In all her search for love, she'd never found one moment of ecstasy, anything that compared to her feelings for Clint.

Chapter Eight

Hearing a car door close, Clint looked out the window and saw Paula heading for the door. Each time he laid eyes on her, he admitted he'd fallen for her. Nosedived was more like it. But today she'd surprised him. She'd never dropped by before without calling. He studied her expression, hoping she wasn't bearing bad news. That was when she seemed to need him most.

He propped the vacuum cleaner against the wall and waited for her steps on the porch. When he opened the door, she threw herself into his arms.

He drew his head back, but seeing her smile, he breathed easier. "You won the lottery."

"Second best. Signed away the house today." She patted her shoulder bag. "The check is right here, and that was followed by a phone call I thought would never come."

The phone call threw him. "Who was it?" He could only think of her missing father or—

"You're looking at an employed woman."

His chest expanded as he tightened his hold around her, lifted her up and spun her into the living room. When he set her down, she reeled a moment with a smile he wanted to keep in his mind forever. "This is a day to mark on the calendar."

She nodded, then gazed around the room. "I hope I'm not interrupting anything."

He chuckled and swung his hand toward the vacuum cleaner. "If you're talking about that, you can interrupt me anytime." He beckoned her deeper into the room. "Have a seat."

She settled onto the sofa as her expression changed. "First, how are you feeling? Better?"

"Much. The cough's nearly gone, and I'll see the doctor in a couple of days. I assume I can get back to work. My energy is up, and my breathing has improved."

"That's wonderful. But I don't want you go back to work too fast, so listen to the doctor."

Her motherly advice tickled him. He'd had no one in recent years who cared one way or the other if he got enough sleep or if he needed a massage for his aching shoulders. "I will. Promise."

Her expression brightened, and she had slipped off her shoes and curled her legs up beneath her, looking as if she spent every evening there by his side.

Warmth swept across his chest and into his heart. This was the kind of relationship he'd dreamed of, one he thought he might have with Elise. Today he wouldn't give a nickel for her. Paula's presence in his life filled him with more than happiness. He felt whole. Complete. His smile could never reflect the joy he felt. Every day was a festive occasion lately when Paula appeared at his door.

"So everything's perfect. You can buy Ashley's home if that's still your plan and still have money to fall back on." If he could keep his financial comments to himself, he'd be happier.

"I definitely want the house. No question, but... everything's not perfect."

His jaw slacked, and he ran his fingers through his hair to keep them busy. He couldn't imagine what wasn't perfect. Rather than trying to guess, he halted his mental acrobatics and rose. "What's the problem?"

"I have thirty days to empty the house. That sounds like a long time, but I start work on Monday. Roscommon is too far to drive there after work, and—"

"Hold on." Relieved, he sank beside her on the sofa, his hand capturing hers. "You have a few days before going to work, and I'm off. Let's start out early tomorrow and see what we can accomplish. You may need help moving things, but you'll know better once you take stock of the situation. It's resolvable."

"You see it clearer than I do. But it's a house full of furniture and piles of memorabilia." She grew silent a moment. "Although I don't really want anything from there."

Her expression caused an ache in his chest. He lifted her hand to his lips and kissed it. "Don't make decisions now. Life has a way of equalizing, and how you feel today doesn't mean you'll feel that way in two weeks or two years."

Silent, she frowned as if implying he had no idea what he was talking about. Still, she might think differently with time. He stifled further comment. "I only mean you can make the decision when we're there. What do you think? Tomorrow?"

"I can't let you tote things to the car, Clint. You're recuperating, and—"

"I'm not a fool. I won't do anything to jeopardize my health. Tomorrow will be an assessment day. Decide if you want anything, otherwise we can make some calls."

She lowered her head, and he could almost hear the gears twirling in her mind. "Assessment only?"

He nodded and raised his hand to his heart. "Promise." Unless she changed her mind.

"Okay." A ragged breath escaped her, and she closed her eyes for a moment. "Clint, I wish I had half the wisdom you have, but I tangle myself in doubts and frustration and get nowhere. I look for the worst. You see the best in almost everything."

She gave him far more credit than he deserved. "Nothing's perfect, Paula, and I'll remind you I'm not perfect, either." He rose and pulled her into his arm.

Her golden-brown eyes searched his, and he melted in their depths. His lips sought hers, and as they kissed, her shoulders relaxed and tension eased from her body. As if they both forgot about their imperfection, their lips melded together in perfect bliss. Their friendship took a giant step forward. This was real. Now all he had to do was convince Paula.

Paula turned the key in the lock and hesitated before she stepped inside her mother's home. Drawing in the moldering air, she made her way inside and wandered through the living room onto the seasonal porch. She stood in silence, looking into the woods where scraggily pines mixed with untamed underbrush. This room, of all in the house, left her with positive memories. Watching nature change seasons, in winter offering the promise of spring and brighter days to come. Within her, those days were now. Her chest tightened, thinking of the changes.

Clint hadn't intruded on her silence, and when she looked behind her, she saw he'd remained near the fireplace. Returning to his side, the dampness in the air sent a shiver rustling down her body, and she covered her arms with her hands, knowing the icy feeling was most likely caused by the house and the dank memories she'd been unable to discard.

"Should I start a fire?" She pointed to the hearth.

Clint checked his watch. "We're leaving in a few hours, and I'd be worried about sparks igniting the carpet once we leave." He craned his neck. "No hearth screen? You— Whoever bought this place should buy one for their own safety."

A chuckle lifted her spirits. "Okay, Mr. Firefighter. I believe you."

Clint looked distracted, his eyes drawn to the mantel. A long-neglected ivy seemed to have caught his eye, and he touched the dried leaves, watching them crumble and fall to the wood. "This reminds me of my mother. She would set dishes of dried flower petals on the foyer table when I lived at home. It left a sweet scent in the air." He ran his free hand through her hair. "Sort of like you."

Her heart lurched, seeing the longing in his eyes.

"I never understood why anyone wanted dried-up flowers, but today…" He drew her closer. "I understand. It reminds us that even things neglected can become beautiful."

The image blossomed in her mind, and his meaning touched her. When she gazed into his eyes, she read more than his words. She knew what she wanted and what he needed. Her pulse sparked as his lips touched hers, a kiss that nearly stopped her heart.

He drew back and shook his head. "I shouldn't have—"

She laid her fingertips against his warm mouth. "No shoulds or shouldn'ts." Her palm grazed across his lips to his cheek and rested against a prickle of whiskers, feeling the warmth of his skin. "You're an amazing man, Clint. I have never been treated with so much respect and kindness in my life."

She understood his discomfort. The kiss had caused them both to yearn for more than a kiss. But never again. What she had with Clint had to be pure and real. For years she'd wanted love so badly she gave in to men's whims, learning each time it only left her feeling unclean and worthless. But Clint lived a life following what he knew God expected. His strong beliefs gave her responsibility to protect them both from a mistake. She saw the warning signal. How long could this go on without ramifications that could hurt them both?

Clint drew in a lengthy breath and stepped away. "What should we do first? You need to decide what you want and then we can make decisions on how to dispose of the rest."

"I don't think I want anything." She eyed him over her shoulder, wanting to talk about what had just happened between them, but she contained the desire. They'd come to the house for a reason, and she would stick to the task. "Should we look in the phone book and find someone to cart it away? That's the quickest and easiest."

Clint turned to her, shaking his head. "Are you purchasing all of Ashley's furniture?"

She rubbed the back of her neck, getting his point. At the moment, she didn't have the finances to buy a house and a houseful of furniture. She dropped her hand and bit the edge of her lip, more confused than she'd been since the day she'd faced caring for her mother. "No, Ashley's keeping a few of her things, but she said I could have what was left if I wanted it."

She suspected Clint needed more convincing. "Remember, Devon's house is completely furnished."

Clint said no more and left her struggling with what to do. Picturing herself living among Ashley's sad memories wasn't much better than existing with her own.

Wrapped in her silent struggle, Clint's voice cut through her concentration. "Paula, I understand why the house brings back bad memories. You told me about the life you led here as a child, but don't let that hold you down. I wish you could give it all to the Lord, but—"

"But I'm a hopeless—"

"Nothing's hopeless." He drew her into his arms again and kissed her hair. "Don't count on Ashley's offer. Devon's home is decorated in his taste…and maybe his former wife's. Ashley might want a lot of her own furniture."

Clint always made sense, although it irked her at times. "I suppose." She gave him that, but she wondered what he'd say if she reminded him her mother had left her tainted by a lifestyle that had affected her life. She'd learned no other way to survive.

She pivoted in a circle and focused on the contents of the living room. Nothing there connected with her. The overstuffed sofa and chairs were worn, and the wood in the other pieces was dark mahogany—too gloomy. She needed brightness in her life for once. "I don't want anything from this room."

"What about the buffet? It's a nice piece of—"

"No." She spun around to face him. "But you know what I'd like?"

He had pulled back as if she'd surprised him. "What?"

"A unit like the one in your house. Oak. You know, with shelves and drawers. It's beautiful and it would be a great addition to the living room."

"I know the one." He chuckled. "Thanks."

She scrutinized him. What had been funny? "Can you remember where you bought it?"

He reached out and drew her closer. "I remember how I got it."

"How?" She studied his face. "You mean—"

"I built it."

She clamped her mouth closed before her jaw dropped, but her surprise couldn't be hidden from him. "You did that? Wow."

His eyes twinkled, but he only shrugged. "It's a hobby."

"It's more than that, Clint. That's what people call a talent."

"Whatever you want to call it, I'll be happy to build anything you want."

"I couldn't ask—"

"I offered, Paula." He gave her a wink. "I'd love to make something for you."

"I love those beautiful doors with inset panels in golden oak?" She pictured him sanding and carving, creating something that lovely, and asked herself what other talents Clint had. What other surprises?

"You tell me. I'll build it."

Her heart lifted as she tiptoed upward to his cheek and kissed it. One thing she knew. This man was nothing like anyone she'd known in her past. Nothing like Vic, for sure. Though she'd known Clint only a short time, he'd grown in stature far more than his powerful frame. He was as unique as the lovely cabinet he'd built.

"Time's fleeting." Clint chucked her under the chin.

"You're right." She walked back onto the porch and examined the two matching rust-colored easy chairs and a golden oak table. This room didn't rile her emotions. The chairs were fairly new, and the table had been a recent addition. She could use those.

When she turned around, Clint had vanished. The furniture slipped onto her mental "take" list before she headed inside, noting the shiny dining-room table in a light-colored wood with black accents. She added that to her list.

A noise sounded from the opposite direction, and she walked down the hallway, passing her mother's room and then the bathroom. Nothing there she wanted. She followed the sound up the staircase. After passing her old bedroom, she found Clint in the room her mother had used for storage but added a sofa bed for guests.

Guests. The word disgusted her.

Clint sat at a table with an album spread in front of him. He swiveled his head toward her when she entered. "I hope you don't mind."

What difference did it make? She shook her head.

"Is this your mother?" He pointed toward one of the photos.

She crossed the room and lowered her eyes to the picture. "She was young then. Probably in her early twenties. I barely remember her like that."

"I can see some of her features in you. She was very pretty, Paula."

Without meaning to, she cringed and wished she hadn't. "I guess she was." The only similarity she could see was their empty lives.

"You'll want to keep these." He dropped it back in a box beside the table and looked up at her. "One day, you may want to show your child what his or her grandmother looked like."

A chill rolled down her back. A child? What was he thinking?

The chair legs scraped against the hardwood floors as he rose.

"I'll never have a—"

"Shh." His lips silenced hers with a tender kiss.

"You can't read the future any more than you can change the past."

She rested her head against his chest as he wrapped his arms around her, protecting her and saving her from sinking. His words lingered in her mind, and she wished she understood how she could give the Lord her burdens and let them go.

"I'd like to understand it all, Clint. I don't know where to begin." She shook her head, frustration filling her face. "I really don't know."

"Scripture and prayer. You can start there. You have the desire, Paula, and that's the hardest part."

Her head spun with warring thoughts, but doubt had no power over her anymore. She wanted to win the battle. Since moving to Ferndale, she'd grown as a person. Hopes and dreams she'd forgotten had come to light, and people she'd met treated her with respect and expectation. It was time she met her own expectations and formed a new life so far from the past she could never go back there again.

Weight lifted from her heart. God or something had answered her needs—the house had sold and she had a new job to start Monday. She stood beside a man who asked nothing of her yet had given her so much. He'd even reminded her she could be a mother one day. She wanted to be a healthy mother. And Clint. He'd be an amazing father.

Hope streamed around her even though it meant telling Clint everything.

Chapter Nine

Time dragged for Clint even though he'd returned to work. The chief put him on limited duty, which meant he stayed at the firehouse, "holding down the fort" as the crew called it, while they went out to fight fires. He'd rather be home than feel useless at the station.

Though assigned to easy tasks, he'd taken it upon himself to add extra jobs to his day, and while he worked, his mind centered on Paula. He'd been to her mother's home twice, and the second time opened his eyes more.

On his first visit, he'd admired the stone fireplace, the open cherrywood staircase and the wide expanse of seasonal porch that gave a great view of the woods, but on his last visit he reevaluated his first impression. His awareness of the damage the environment had brought to Paula changed his perception.

This time he noticed the beige walls, white draperies at the windows and the furniture upholstery a darker beige. The wooden floors throughout most of the house and no pictures or decorations to add color took life from the rooms. The ivy had died and crumbled at his touch. Lifeless. That's what he'd call it. Even a hospital room had a bulletin board and a wall clock.

Though he was considered to be a strong, rugged male, the word *cozy* had meaning for him. The house in Roscommon lacked warmth—nothing there left him with a comfortable feeling. The dankness of the rooms echoed the spiritless life still hanging in the air. Picturing Paula growing up in the environment with her mother's immoral existence helped him understand the lack of love she'd felt.

No wonder she'd been hesitant to take a leap of faith. She'd watched her mother fail at relationships, and he understood why Paula might envision herself in that situation. That's what she'd learned. Man-hopping. The idea dug deep into the pit of his gut. He couldn't imagine Paula with that mind-set. Certainly she had more intelligence than to slip into the mire of her mother's lifestyle. His desire to show her what great things life could offer choked his heart. His determination had grown beyond his ability to hold it back.

An uneasy thought came to him. In that horrific environment for a young girl, could something have happened to her in that house? Images flashed in his mind of her innocence being ripped away by one of the lowlifes her mother had allowed into their home. Into their home with no regard for a young daughter just blossoming into womanhood. His chest ached with concern. Could this be the ugly part of her life that held her back and made her feel less than worthy? His disgust grew as his fist knotted.

He could never ask. Never. Yet it made him long all the more to rescue her, to help her know in her heart that she was as pure as the morning dew.

He was committed. He'd finally met a woman he wanted to be with, a woman he could marry, but... she'd said it herself. He knew what the Bible taught, and despite his feelings, he had some reluctance to continue in a relationship leading to marriage when the woman didn't embrace his faith.

A ragged breath tore through his chest, leaving an ache reminiscent of the pain he experienced after the smoke inhalation. He closed the magazine and tossed it aside, frustrated with being treated as an invalid. He lowered his eyelids, his supplication filling his mind. But prayers had rattled in his head so often he wondered if God got tired of hearing the same pleas.

His cell phone came to life, and his heart lurched. Paula was the only one who called him these days, and he hadn't heard from her since returning to work. She tended to hesitate, fearing she would interrupt his work. But since returning, his work had involved menial tasks.

Picturing her at the other end of the call lifted his

spirit. He pulled the phone from his pocket, and then his mind flew back in time. While his pulse skittered, he stared at the phone, unable to answer. Finally catching his breath, he hit the button. "Elise?"

"Clint, it's been a long time. How are you?"

"Fine. What's up?"

She didn't respond for a moment, but he heard her breathing. "I surprised you, I suppose?"

She supposed? That was an understatement. "I'm at the station, Elise. Can I help you?"

"No, but I had hoped you'd be happy to hear from me."

He pulled back the phone and stared at it. Was she insane? "Surprised."

"I'm sorry, Clint. I suppose you're married and I shouldn't—"

"I'm not married, but I'm curious why you're calling me."

"So you are single." Her tone had lifted. "So am I."

Huh? The purpose for her phone call struck him in the gut and sickened him. "I'm sorry." He'd stretched the truth. She deserved every miserable moment of her life. "You're divorced, I assume."

"The marriage was a mistake, Clint. It was my second big error."

He pictured her blond hair brushing her shoulders, her fluttering lashes and her tapered nose that turned upward at the end. She'd captured him once but not again. "We all make mistakes. We learn from them and grow." From the sound of her voice, he suspected she'd found herself stuck in the same hole she'd been in when she walked away from their wedding.

"That's why I decided to come home for a while."

He could only shake his head and swallow the bile rising to his throat. The best he could do with her call was to gain a sense of closure, but lately he'd realized that wasn't important anymore. Paula had reminded him that he wasn't likely the one with the problem. That's all he'd needed to hear. And today, in his eyes, Elise had validated it.

"Clint?"

Her plaintive voice tripped to his ear. "Yeah?"

"I thought maybe we'd been cut off."

"No. I'm busy, Elise. I'm at work." He'd stretched another truth. Sitting and looking at an old magazine he'd probably read before didn't meet the definition of busy.

"All right. This was bad timing. I should have known." Silence inched along until he heard her breathe. "I'll say goodbye for now."

He heard the disconnect and released a stream of air, but as he did, her words came back to him. *I'll say goodbye for now.* He'd been miserable all day, wanting to get back to work—real work instead of babysitting the station. Her call made everything else seem insignificant. She'd riled the confusion he'd lugged around for too long. Firefighters had a lifestyle some women couldn't handle, and he'd learned that now. He'd watched some marriages crumble, but not for his buddies not trying.

He buried his face in his hands, hoping to dispel the tension that had raked through him, leaving a sting. At one time, he'd thought seeing her had value. Though Elise had reappeared, he knew better now. Something more important needed his efforts rather than swathing an old ache. His relationship with Paula had just begun to strengthen. And now Elise had fallen into the picture. He had no control over Elise and what she really wanted or what she might do.

"Clint, if you're not feeling well, you need to go home."

His head snapped up, hearing Devon's voice.

"No, I'm okay." He straightened in the chair and planted a pleasant expression on his face. At least he hoped that was what it was.

"We can manage here, pal." Devon rested his hand on Clint's shoulder. "I feared you would come back too soon. You're a hard worker, but you should take care of yourself first."

"I'm fine, Dev. Well, I was fine until..." Too late to keep his mouth shut. He'd flapped his jaw and sucking back the words couldn't be done. He needed to think the situation through on his own without anyone's opinion to sway what he needed to do.

Devon's face screwed into a quizzical expression. "Until what?"

"Until Elise called."

Devon's eyes opened as wide as his mouth. "You're kidding." He shook his head. "No, I don't suppose you'd kid about that." He grasped a chair back as if to steady himself. "What did she want?"

Clint rolled his eyes. "I have no idea except she's divorced and thought I'd be happy to hear from her."

"Ah. That's rather open-ended."

"She said she was coming back home for a while to deal with her mistakes. I didn't want to hear anymore. I told her I was at work and ended the call, but not before I heard her last line." He shook his head, choking on the words. "She said, 'I'll say goodbye for now.'"

Devon seemed frozen in place. "For now, huh?" Finally, he came back to life. "You don't look happy."

"Should I be?"

He drew up his shoulders and shrugged. "That's up to you."

Clint didn't know how to respond, and he certainly hadn't expected Devon to say something like that. "That's been long over, Dev. I thought once I'd like to have her explain, but you know what? It doesn't matter anymore."

"Good for you." He gave Clint a wink. "I'm guessing my sort-of sister-in-law can take credit for some of that."

Clint winked back. "Wouldn't you like to know?"

Devon let out a horselaugh and strutted away.

Clint watched him go, wishing he could laugh about the situation, but Elise's goodbye gave him concern.

"Are you sure this covers everything?" She eyed Ashley and Devon, trying to read their expressions. "The check is half of the value—my down payment—and I'll make monthly installments for—"

"It's more than half, Paula." Devon eyed the check. "We're not taking money for the furniture. Those things are a gift from Ashley until you can replace them with your own purchases. Then you can sell the items or donate them to charity. They belong to you."

"But the appliances and—"

"How many stoves and refrigerators does one person need?" Ashley shook her head and chuckled. "Devon has a new fridge and he put his old one in the basement for extra storage. We don't want another stove."

Paula's chest constricted. "Thanks. You've done more than I could ever imagine."

"You're family—like a sister. We love you."

Ashley's words washed over her as comforting as a warm bath. "I've decided to bring a few things from Mother's house. Clint insisted, and he was right."

They did a double take. She was sure she'd mentioned it…or Clint would have.

"How are you moving the items here?" Devon stuffed the check into his wallet.

"I hired a guy to move it here. The rest is going to charity." Her chest tightened again, but this time with concern. She'd only talked with Clint once since he'd brought her back from Roscommon. Part of their distance had been her reluctance to get any more involved than she already was. Things were moving too fast.

Devon rose. "Let us know if you need help. I'm off Sunday and Monday." He tilted his head back. "I suppose Monday won't work now with your job."

"I know. The house sale and the job came at the same time, but I'm not complaining. I'm grateful."

Ashley came to her side and kissed her cheek. "We're both happy for you."

"I know you are." She rose and gave her cousin a hug. "Thanks. You're making my dream came true."

"We're glad." Devon squeezed her arm and headed toward the kitchen.

But Ashley paused. "Dad said you've been reading the Bible."

A lump caught in Paula's throat, and she could only nod.

"I'm happy you are." Her mouth curved upward. "If you have any questions—"

"Your dad's been good about answering the ones I've had. He suggested I read the New Testament first." She studied Ashley's expression and got positive feedback.

She finally nodded. "You're surprising me, Paula, and yet, it's so good. I'm really happy that you're taking this step." She gave a wave and headed toward the door but slowed and turned to her again. "If you want to go to church with us, just let me know."

"Thanks." She watched Ashley vanish around the corner. Their footsteps faded as they exited.

She rubbed her face and sank into the chair again, taking a moment to put her checkbook into her shoulder bag. So many things were falling into place except the one major decision she'd made, and that one broke her heart. Falling in love, she'd learned, wasn't something that could be controlled. It happened whether the person wanted it to or not, and she'd let it sneak up on her. But for now the emotion had to be put in bubble wrap and placed somewhere safe until she knew faith was possible for her. She owed it to Clint.

Prayer had happened without thinking once she'd realized that she couldn't make a mistake with prayer. If there was a God, he'd hear it, and if there wasn't, then it didn't make a difference, but lately when she prayed, she'd been washed in a sense of comfort. She couldn't stop the feeling, and the more she prayed and read the Bible, the more she'd faced a truth she hadn't considered. Her cousins and uncle weren't gullible people. Clint was as far from being duped as many might be. And they believed without a doubt. She'd heard it in their conversations and prayers at dinner. She'd seen it in their actions.

Those seeds inside her that Clint had mentioned had burst open, and tendrils of faith had begun to wind around her heart and through her being. She had changed, desiring to pray rather than wishing she could.

The doorbell chimed and she stilled, not wanting to deal with anyone at the moment. Then she remembered her uncle had gone somewhere with Alice—their time together had become more frequent—which meant she was the only one home to answer. She rose to deal with the door and pulled the latch.

Clint stood on the other side, one hand on the screen door handle and another clutching a bouquet of flowers. His serious expression gave her concern.

"Are you home?"

His silly question eased her tension. "No, but come in anyway." She pushed the screen door forward as he pulled. "Is someone sick?" She nodded toward the flowers, hoping to make him smile.

He did. "I am, but I bought these for you." He handed her the bouquet wrapped in florist paper and tied with a ribbon.

"If I didn't know better, I'd wonder if these are a peace offering" She cradled the bouquet. "Or maybe it's a ploy to cover your guilt about something. I've read articles about that in magazines. Never trust a bouquet of roses."

"They're not roses." Though he chuckled, she sensed something was askew.

Without probing him, she headed to the kitchen to find a vase, and he followed her. He'd never given her flowers before although he'd done so much more. Still, the beautiful bouquet made her think.

She opened the cabinet door, closed it and opened the next. On the top shelf, she spotted a vase tall enough to hold the long stems. "Can you reach that?" She pointed to the glass container too high for her to reach.

He lifted it down, and she filled it with water from the tap. When she set the vase on the counter, he had already untied the ribbon and unbound the bouquet from the floral paper. She gazed at the lovely blossoms—colorful snapdragons, pink carnations, yellow poms and blue iris. Withdrawing the green ferns and purple statice first, she arranged them in the vase, then added the flowers to form a balanced display of height and color. She stood back, admiring her handiwork.

"Talk about creative." Clint held the vase in his hand, turning it to view from all sides. "This is really pretty, Paula. Done like a pro."

Humbled by the memory of his amazing woodwork, she thanked him and carried the arrangement back into the living room and placed it on the table in front of the picture window.

"Have a seat." She gestured to the sofa where he

usually sat, and she sank into the easy chair near him. He looked pale, taking her back to his time in the hospital. "How are you feeling now that you're working again?"

His expression answered her question, and she understood even more when he explained his limited duty and boredom, but she sensed he had more on his mind and suspected it was about her. "I didn't want to call you at work since you'd been gone all those days. I figured it would be an adjustment and—"

"That's okay. I understand. I think the real issue is we were both thoughtful when we got back from Roscommon, and we were uncomfortable with what happened between us." He captured her gaze. "At least I was."

Blunt and to the point. Here it came. She shifted her eyes from his. She'd feared this from day one, and with Clint, she recognized bad news even before he expressed it. "That's part of it, I guess." She forced herself to look at him. "I've been thinking a lot, and I—"

"And you don't want to see me anymore."

Sadness filled his face. His reaction startled her, and it made her ache. "No, that's not it. Not at all."

His back straightened, and though his expression held concern, his eyes glinted hope. "What is it then?"

"I'm going to be open with you, Clint. If I were

ready to make a commitment, you'd be the only man who'd make me want to take that step."

His dazed eyes searched hers. "Then what's the but?"

"You and I know what happened when you kissed me in Roscommon." Grateful that he nodded, she didn't need to explain her meaning. She wrapped her mind around the rest of her thoughts. "But I know intimacy isn't what you want outside of marriage." She studied his expression for validation. "I know I'm right about that."

His face tensed again, causing her concern, but he didn't falter. "You are right, and I know that's why we were uneasy, but that being said, I need to disappoint you here."

A hollow feeling depleted the air in her lungs.

"When I was in my early twenties, I knew what was right, but I did get that involved with a girl. It seemed every guy I knew had a story to tell, and I began to wonder if I was the only twenty-two-year-old virgin in the state."

Though he grimaced, she had to hold back a nervous laugh. In other circumstances, what he said might have held humor. But not now. "I admit I'm surprised."

"I never wanted to lead you on. I'm not perfect. I've made mistakes and without the excuse of ignorance. I knew I was doing wrong, but I did it anyway. It took me a long time to forgive myself even though I knew the Lord had forgiven me the moment I faced the truth and I regretted what I'd allowed to happen."

She considered this idea, recalling scripture relating stories of Jesus forgiving great sins out of love. Could that be the situation in her case? Had God forgiven her, but she hadn't forgiven herself?

Her own admission hung by a thread in her mind, a thread ready to break with the weight of her sorrow. Clint had confessed his sin, and it was time for her to tell him everything. She gazed at the lovely bouquet of bright colors and sweet scent. They would shrivel and die without water, and so would her relationship with Clint without truth, but the admission sucked the life from her.

"What's wrong, Paula?" He blew out a stream of air. "I'm sorry I've disappointed you."

The sadness in his voice startled her. "You haven't disappointed me, Clint. I've disappointed myself far more than you could ever upset me." She steeled herself. "Since we're being honest, let me expand on my story." She forced herself to look into his eyes.

He didn't blink but leaned closer, resting his elbows on his knees. "Please. I want to know everything about you."

Not this, but it was time. "I told you about my mother, but I'm no better, Clint. I didn't think of my body as sacred. I'd never even thought like that. I saw it as a way to find love. That's what my mother did. Or I thought she'd found love. What she'd found was security and a man to hold her in his arms. I wasn't naive. I knew what went on, and though it disgusted me to one extent, it answered my desire to be loved...or what I thought would be love."

His breath rattled from his chest. She closed her eyes, fearing that he would stand and walk away, but when she lifted her eyelids, he was still there. As she opened her mouth, she feared telling him everything. He'd told her about one girl, and her admission was worse and could destroy the progress they'd made in their relationship.

But she'd opened the subject and so she continued and told Clint about the night she met Vic. "He came off as a gentleman. He never tried anything. He didn't ask for anything from me. That night he drove me home and kissed my cheek at the door." She shook her head, still unable to wrap the image around her mind. "Can you understand how amazing that was for me?"

Clint gave a faint nod, his expression rapt in her experience.

"After a couple of weeks, he gave me a bottle of perfume and told me how much I meant to him. He'd been looking for work, and meanwhile he was staying with friends. Since I had an apartment to myself, I invited him to move there until he got his life in order." Her stomach knotted remembering that day. "Clint, I had dreams. Hopes. Vic sounded grateful and moved in with a small suitcase and a mouthful of thank-yous."

The rest of the story curdled, and she spoke it

into the air, more to persuade herself than Clint how she'd fallen prey to a liar. She'd become a victim of— She closed her eyes, dispelling her excuses. She'd been utterly desperate for love.

"Then it happened. Vic was short of money, and I gave him a loan. Soon he had my credit card and took money as he needed it. I didn't bat an eye. I responded like a wife. He came home with gifts for me and groceries occasionally, and I didn't give a thought to what was really happening."

Clint made a groaning sound. "So he was buying you presents and supplies with your money."

"Not only that, Clint. I was so stupid and trusting that I didn't even check my financial records. For the first time in my life, I had a person who came home to me at night—sometimes later than I wanted—but he came home, and I thought he loved me. I talked about making it legal, and he said not until he found a job and made things right."

"But he found no job?" Clint shook his head, concern etching his face.

"No job, but he was getting a sturdy bank balance. He was stealing my savings, and I didn't see it. By then he'd taken over paying the bills and depositing my checks at the bank for me. I was duped. Horribly and stupidly duped. A woman of thirty who had the brain of a teenager." Her voice caught in her throat. "But a hunger for love can do that."

Clint rose and drew her into his arms. Instead of

disgust, his face churned with a look of indignation. "He wasn't a man, Paula. He was scum. Good-looking maybe, but beneath it scum."

"But I was old enough to know better."

"Age had nothing to do with it. You had no one who demonstrated what a healthy relationships should be. How could you not look to your mother for an example and think you were—"

"If I really search inside me, I did know something was wrong. I just didn't want to face it." Her chest ached holding back the anger she felt for Vic and the disgust she held for herself. "I looked at my friends with healthy relationships—the few I had— and they had concerns, but I defended him." Pain knotted in her neck and radiated down her back. "I didn't want to face reality. I didn't want to admit I'd been gullible and stupid."

He drew back, his eyes searching hers. "Are you sick? You don't look well."

"It's nothing. I've dreaded telling you this, and I don't know how you can—"

He kissed her cheek and eased her into the chair, then stood behind her, massaging her neck and shoulders until the tension lessened and she could breathe again.

"Better?"

She nodded, not wanting him to stop. She'd spewed the story, and instead of turning his back, he'd sided with her, found excuses and spoken his concern. She didn't deserve one minute of his kindness. He'd done what he'd told her God did for His children. The example warmed her heart.

Clint gave her back a final rub and rounded the chair. "Thank you for telling me. It breaks my heart, Paula, but you don't need anyone's forgiveness except your own. You've already atoned. I can hear that in your voice, and if I can hear it, you know the Lord can. It's all in your hands now."

"And you're not disappointed? Disgusted?"

"No more than I am with myself." He wandered back to the sofa and sank into the cushion. He studied her a moment, his expression morphing from one emotion to the other until she stopped trying to read his thoughts. When he leaned forward, he rested his elbows on his knees, his hands folded. "But what I need to know now is where do we stand?"

His question came out of the blue. Or did it? She thought back to the beginning of their conversation. "You mean our friendship?"

"Friendship." His jaw tightened. "Is that really what it is?" His eyes told the truth.

"No. It's far more than friendship alone, Clint. You're my breath of life, my hope for the future, my inspiration."

"Then what's holding us back from making a—"

She pressed the flat of her hand against her chest. "Me."

Confusion covered his face, his eyes searching hers in silence.

"Until I can be a woman that will make you happy, one who fits your life and faith, I can't take that step. You deserve to be a father, Clint, but I'm not sure I can be a good mother. I can't deprive you of that joy. I would never forgive myself."

"But—"

She stopped him with a flex of her hand. "No buts. You said I had the seeds, Clint, and I trust that you're right. I've seen the tiny buds of faith form. Now I'm waiting for them to open. You reminded me that you can't do it for me. I have to not only open my mind but also my heart. So much of my life has changed, even blossomed, so those buds could blossom, too. It just takes time."

"Time." He rose and knelt beside her. He drew her hand to his lips and kissed it. "I can wait."

Her breathing ceased, and she gulped for air. "You're willing to wait?"

"I am." He rose and drew her into an embrace. "I know those special kisses will have to be saved for later, but I can still touch your lips with mine and hold you."

He slipped his arms around her and drew her close, his lips brushing hers with the gentleness of a summer breeze.

Joy rippled through her, a shudder he felt by his loving touch. "Thank you."

He rested his cheek on hers, his hand flowing

down her back like raindrops on a window. "I can wait as long as it takes."

Her arms trembled as he pressed her to his heart, and she prayed.

Chapter Ten

"What do you think?" Paula stood back and studied the blue-and-rust upholstery of the sofa Ashley had left behind, which was positioned near the two rust chairs Paula had taken from her mother's all-season porch. Together it gave both of them new life.

"It looks great." Ashley slipped her arm around her shoulders. "In fact, it looks as if you bought the pieces together. I never liked the look of chairs I'd used in the room, but then I was grateful for any furniture. Adam had received notice of duty in the Middle East, and my mind had been focused on that."

Her voice had trailed off, and Paula's lungs pushed against her heart. She couldn't imagine. "I'm surprised you were able to do anything." Then it hit her. "And you'd just learned you were pregnant."

Ashley nodded. "We were thrilled to leave the apartment and have our own home with our first baby on the way. We thought everything was perfect, and then…"

She didn't need to finish the sentence. "I'm always wary when things seem perfect, Ash. Somehow the ax always falls."

Ashley nodded. "I know." She sank into one of the rust chairs, rubbing her fingers over the nappy fiber. "Like now."

Paula's breath hitched. "What's wrong, Ash?"

She gave Paula a strange look. "I'm talking about Clint's situation."

"Clint's situation?" She stared at Ashley, uncertain of what she meant.

Ashley's eyes widened, and she slapped her hand over her mouth. "Oh, Paula. I'm so sorry." She lowered her head and shook it. "I don't think Clint told you."

Her pulse exploded. "Told me what?"

Ash's head inched upward. "Elise."

Paula suspected her face had turned as pale as Ashley's. "What about her?"

"She's coming back to Ferndale. Her parents still live here."

Her mind spinning, Paula sank onto the sofa. Clint hadn't told her. That had to mean it was something he didn't want her to know. But why?

"I could kick myself." Ashley rose. "I'm so sorry." She rattled a sigh. "I'm sure he didn't mention it because he didn't want to stir up your worries when everything was going so well for you."

"But I'd want to know. Don't make excuses for him." She fought tears attacking her eyes. "Anyway, we don't have a commitment. Nothing. He—"

"What are you talking about?" Ashley darted from the chair and caved onto the cushion beside her. "Words don't make a commitment. Your actions do. Clint hasn't dated since I've known him, and Devon said he never knew the guy to go out with anyone after Elise walked out on him. Clint wouldn't even go to a movie with Devon or stop for breakfast when they left the station." She grasped Paula's hand. "He's been like a new man since you stepped into his life."

Nothing stirred hope in her. She'd been a distraction while he waited for Elise. "If I mean something to him, he should have confided in me. Not in you and—"

"Devon told me how upset Clint was. Clint never said a word to me, Paula. Not one word."

She replayed their last conversation. She'd confessed her disgusting life, and he'd guaranteed her that it made no difference. Later when it sank in, who knew what would happen? She'd been surprised at his confession, but that hadn't been as shameful her million-dollar admission. She'd sinned, and the sin left her used and dirty.

Clint had been upset, but he blamed Vic and excused her. She remembered his words when she asked if he were disappointed or disgusted. He'd said, "No more than I am with myself." But what did that mean? If he still harbored disgust for his own sin, then he certainly harbored disgust for hers.

She'd seen his expression when he arrived...and the flowers. She'd made a joke about guilt. Maybe it wasn't a joke after all.

The picture twisted in her mind. Was it guilt? He would feel guilt if he'd planned to tell her that Elise had returned and he was going back to their relationship. Or was he upset because Elise had stirred up a problem when his life seemed perfect? *Perfect.* The word sickened her. She tossed the options in her head. Which way did it go?

Ashley stood again and walked to the window. "When the guys get back, I'm telling Clint what I've done, and hope that he'll forgive me."

"Please don't bring it up, Ash. Let me talk with him. I'll let him know your reference was a mistake. That you assumed I knew." She stood and dragged herself to the window beside her. "It's not your fault. An honest man would have told me."

"Honest? Clint's the most honest man I know. Let him explain. Don't assume you know what was in his mind or why he didn't bring it up. People are innocent until proven guilty."

She snapped her head around to face Ashley. "Do you know how many people get away with murder?"

Ashley's color drained. Tears flooded her eyes, and she spun around and darted through the front door. She watched as Ashley hurried down the road toward home. Though she didn't know for sure, Paula assumed Ashley could not forgive herself for opening up something Clint had been hiding from her. She didn't blame Ashley but she supposed her own over the top reaction threw Ashley off. Why would she ever compare Clint's indiscretion to getting away with murder? She and Clint had no agreement, nothing that would keep him from going back to…Elise. Still, the thought tore her to pieces.

Paula sank into the chair, her mind reeling, her spirit boiling with despair. *Why Lord? Are You listening? Are You even there?*

Clint sat frozen to the spot. He peeled his fingers from the steering wheel, the bag of fast food sitting in Devon's lap. A rush of fear roared in his ears when Ashley flagged them down on the street.

"Clint, I'm sorry. So sorry." Tears rolled down her eyes.

"What? What happened?" His heart raced. "Is it Paula? What happened?"

"I didn't know you hadn't mentioned Elise's call, and…"

His stomach knotted, and her mistake hit home. He'd been stupid to avoid telling her. As he listened to her spill out the story, he realized that Paula had drawn an assumption that was so far from the truth he couldn't see it. Elise meant nothing to him but a pain that he'd allowed to fester until he'd come to his senses. He'd done that with Paula's help. Nothing could influence him to take a second look at Elise.

He studied Ashley's pale face and tear-filled eyes, and he knew how she felt. "It's not your fault, Ash. I should have told her. I'd convinced myself that not knowing would alleviate her concerns. Things have been great for her. Selling her mother's house, getting the job, realizing she has a second chance for a better life, everything had worked out. I've been happy beyond words noticing the changes in her. Telling her would have been a setback."

The reasoning split him in two. "But that was my error." He looked down the street toward Paula's new house and struggled to calm himself. "Let me go there alone. Just for a few minutes. I'll call you when—"

Devon grasped his arm and gave it a squeeze. "Take your time. We'll save the burgers for you."

"I couldn't eat now if I had to." Shaking his head, Clint rubbed his pounding temple.

Devon slipped from the passenger seat and rounded the car. He leaned into the driver's window with Ashley by his side, her face still stained with tears. "I'll be praying, Dev." Ashley gave a nod and buried her face in Devon's shoulder.

"Thanks for the prayers." Clint lifted his foot from the brake and rolled down the street, his heart in his throat. Every excuse that ran through his mind sounded wimpy. Telling her would have made sense.

He saw it now. It could have solidified their relationship instead of tearing it apart.

Pulling into the driveway, he collected his thoughts and drew on his inner strength. The truth made sense. No excuses. She'd know if he was hedging. He turned the key and pulled it from the ignition, letting his back flop against the seat. Lord. He swallowed his words. God knew his heart and that's all he needed to say.

He stood at the side door, tossing the options of ringing the bell or just walking in. The question wasn't needed. He grasped the knob, turned it and climbed the two stairs to the kitchen. He paused, not knowing which way to turn, but he took a chance and swung through the dining room into the living room.

Paula looked up, her eyes glazed and her face tight with anguish. Awareness flashed in her eyes. "She told you."

He heard her ragged sigh.

"I understand, Clint. Please don't drag me through your excuses. We made no commitment, no promises. You're free to live your life as you please."

He moved closer. "Thank you, Paula. I'm relieved you feel that way."

Her eyes didn't blink, her face stoic. She'd fallen back into the Paula he'd met what seemed like years ago. Finally, she gave a faint nod.

Instead of walking away as she must have expected, he stepped toward her, drew her into his arms and crushed her to his chest. "This is what I want, Paula. I had no decision to make."

Confusion flooded her face, her eyes searching his in a dazed stare.

Despite their agreement, he tossed it aside and lowered his mouth to hers, every ounce of longing washing over him, drenching his heart with something he'd longed for but never had until she stepped into his life.

Her body stiffened against his, her mouth pulling away, but undaunted, he held her fast, praying the Lord open her eyes. Her rigid stance diminished, and she yielded to his strength as if she could no longer stand on her own. When he eased back, the same confusion flickered in her eyes but, with it, a seeming willingness to listen.

He slipped his hand in hers and guided her to the sofa, where he sat beside her and held her in his arms. Silence covered them while the air snapped with anticipation.

In the quiet, her breathing slowed while his pulse eased to a trot. "I know you don't want excuses and I won't give you any. Only an explanation."

She studied him a moment before drawing back and sinking into the cushion.

"It was a phone call, Paula. She called and I was shocked." He explained the conversation and his disgust in her purpose for calling. He could only assume that she thought he'd stumble back to her, filled with forgiveness, maybe even on his knees, offering her love and security. "She has nothing to offer me, Paula. I have everything I want."

Her eyes searched his before focusing across the distance. He feared her thoughts were there, too, dredging up the horrors of her past or putting him in the same category as Vic or one of the other men who'd stolen her life from her.

He didn't give up. "I promised I would wait, and I'm keeping that promise. I know trusting is hard for you, but you've seen me in action and I pray one day you'll accept my word and trust me."

Her mouth pulled at the corners, and he longed to see her smile, to cover her with kisses and to hear her say he was forgiven.

"I need time to weigh the situation, Clint. I know I'm always asking for time, but if we have any hope of resolution, that's what I need."

"I promised to wait, and I will no matter what the reason. I'm in no hurry."

"Thank you." She leaned closer and brushed her lips against his.

"That's all I needed." Though only a whisper in her hair, his voice resounded in the heavy quiet.

Clint leaned back and chuckled when he saw Devon. "Guess what I found in my wallet?"

"Hundred-dollar bill?"

"Not quite." He flipped open his billfold and pulled out the card. "It's our win from the Sequence game."

Devon eyed his prize. "You haven't used it."

He gazed at the gift card for Clawson Steak House. "I forgot." He grinned at Devon, shaking his head. "I know. I've been on a short thread lately."

"Maybe it's good you still have it. You owe that lovely lady a night out."

Clint thought of the mess created by Elise's phone call and gave Devon a thumbs-up.

Sal appeared over his shoulder. "You still have that thing. If you don't want it, Maureen loves the place." He gave Clint's back a pat before extending his hand.

"No luck, pal. Think of it as spent. Friday night, if that works for Paula." He slipped the card back into his wallet. "Paula deserves a fun night out as a celebration of her new house." He looked at Sal over his shoulder. "Thanks to Ashley and Devon."

Devon's voice sailed from the other side of the room. "Don't thank us. Paula paid our asking price and selling it to her saved us all kinds of costs. We owe her our thanks."

"But a home of her own is something she's dreamed about. Seeing her happy makes me happy."

Sal's chuckle reverberated behind him. "The boy's got it bad."

Cringing, Clint clamped his mouth closed, surprised he'd said so much.

When the others went on to their evening activities, he settled into an easy chair and pulled out his cell phone. He loved his work, but for the first time in his life, he missed being home. He missed Paula.

Their relationship hadn't been smooth. He would never say it had been, and they still faced bumpy roads. She needed time, and he understood. At one time, he'd needed the same, but not anymore. If he were sure of anything, he knew how he felt about her.

Her lack of faith hadn't been a concern until his heart took over and he realized what that meant. A proposal. Marriage. That was on hold. But he still believed that a person's actions could influence others, and he'd never hidden his faith from anyone. She'd witnessed it and even commented that she wished she had something to lean on. He'd offered his shoulder, but his shoulder was aeons from God's power. Paula had needed to know that the Lord loved her and was there for her, no matter what. And now even he'd witnessed evidence of her growing faith.

The seeds had been planted, but he'd helped her become aware of them. That's all he'd done. Nothing more. Yet her drive and desire to learn had been watered by others, and here she was today, seeming more and more to grow, to pray and to study the Word.

Every day he became more confident their lives were lining up and one day she'd let him know she could accept what he had to offer, a life with him. Children? The longing to be a father swelled in his heart, and despite Paula's fears that she'd be a terrible mother, he had no doubt she had learned from her mother's mistakes. People could learn from bad experiences and she would provide the opposite lifestyle for her children—one filled with love, security and laughter. Paula would be a wonderful mother.

His cheeks felt the pull of a smile, and he glanced around the room, hoping no one noticed him grinning like an idiot as he sat alone staring into space. He looked behind him, half expecting Sal to be lurking nearby, but he was alone in his corner, and he raised his cell phone and punched in Paula's number.

He listened to it ring—three, four, five—until voice mail kicked in. Disappointed, he ended the call and slipped the phone into his shirt pocket. He sat a moment, trying to get his mind on something else. An idea struck him, and he hoisted himself from the chair and headed toward the door, deciding to hit the exercise room. Before he got through the door, a vibration quivered against his chest followed by the familiar ring tone. He tugged the phone from his pocket, and Paula's name appeared.

Wanting privacy, he pivoted around as he answered and returned to his corner. His disappointment fading, he sank into the chair. "Busy?"

"I'd left my phone in the living room. When you called, I was on the kitchen floor."

"The floor?"

Paula chuckled. "Sorting through pans and casserole dishes. How many of those things does one person need?"

He shrugged, shaking his head at the uselessness of his visual response. "You lost me there. You know I'm not a great cook." He spotted Devon coming through the doorway and knew he needed to get down to business. He turned his back, hoping he could finish before Devon got too close. "I found the gift card today from the Sequence party. How about dinner on Friday night? We can celebrate your pan arrangement or the new house and use the card at the same time."

"Multitasking. Ingenuous."

"Thanks."

"You're welcome, and I'd be honored to accept your dinner celebration."

His pulse hitched facing the questions he didn't want to ask. They were hedging on responses he might not want to hear. The warning failed. "How's it going?"

Silence.

He knew it. One day he'd learn to keep his mouth closed. For most people that would mean nothing, but for Paula his question held an innuendo.

"Getting things organized and put away I rank about a B plus." Silence. "And my messed-up head? I'm getting it together inch by inch. Grade—improving."

Grateful for her upbeat response, he decided to

proceed. "Great on both counts, Paula, and I'm sorry I asked the question that way."

"It's not you. It's me, Clint. You know that. Until I view things through new eyes, I'm a real pain. I'm not sure what you see in me."

Her image filled his heart. "Your hair glowing in the sunlight, your smile that lights my world, your kisses warming my heart, your wit making me laugh, your—"

"Whoa. I have to observe this myself, and there's no mirror in this room. I don't want to miss this illusion you're having."

Gooseflesh prickled his arms. "I wish I could be there to see you in person." When had he become Robert Browning, gushing love phrases?

Her chuckle awakened him, and he saw Devon with his usual taunting grin heading toward him. "I smell smoke. I'd better hang up."

"Really?" Concern rattled her voice.

"No, but I'm on fire." Heat rose up his collar, and he craned his neck to make sure no one heard his ridiculous words.

"Silly. I'll see you on…"

"Thursday after I catch forty winks, and don't forget our date on Friday." He opened his mouth to say he loved her, then slammed it closed. He managed a goodbye.

Devon stopped to talk to one of the crew, giving Clint time to sit a moment, amazed at what he'd heard spewing from his mouth. Mr. Rescuer, Mr.

Firefighter, Mr. Confident, Mr. Reliable and— He snapped his mind shut. He'd lost it. Over the edge. Out on a limb.

Lord, this is in Your hands.

Chapter Eleven

Paula waited for Clint to open the car door as he always did. From the day she'd met him, he'd made her feel special. Yet accepting it had taken time. She'd finally come to grips with all he'd opened to her, a life she'd never known, and a real man who'd helped her see the true meaning of trust and hope.

The door opened, and she shifted, slipping her feet to the ground. She stepped out of the way as he closed the door. Instead of moving inside, he gazed at her a moment, his look tender and engrossing. Air emptied from her chest with an overwhelming awe of him. He'd dressed in gray pants and a navy jacket with a gray-and-blue tie. His dark hair looked so full she longed to run my fingers through it.

Linking his arm with hers, he guided her inside the stone and white stucco building, where the hostess led them to a table set with white linen near the bandstand. Clint rolled back the white upholstered chair as she sloughed off her coat, and when she sat, he settled adjacent to her, both facing the bandstand.

"I didn't know they had music." She eyed the white sparkling background framing the name, Mark James Band.

"They begin at eight. We'll stick around for a while." He eased his hand toward hers and covered it with his palm.

The vision of their first meeting, when she was uncomfortable and unsure, shifted to days and weeks when she tried to avoid falling in love. The images spiraled around her, a kaleidoscope of experience that left her dazed.

"Remember our first date?" Clint's question chased away the quiet.

"How could I forget? I remember everything." His fingers wove through hers, sparking warm recollections. "Even the day we went to the park."

He chuckled. "But the crowd scared—"

"Welcome to Clawson Steak House. I'm Rose, your server. Are you ready to order?"

Her head jerked up and she grasped the menu, sending the waitress a feeble grin.

The woman caught on and smiled. "What would you like to drink?"

Clint ordered two coffees, then picked up the menu as the waitress left. "Everything is good here. This is the only place I know that begins the meal with soup and salad, plus great bread."

"I'll be full by the time the meal arrives." She

lifted the folder and gazed at the long list of choices, deciding on the sautéed lake perch while Clint opted for the horseradish-encrusted salmon.

After they placed their order, a waiter filled their water glasses, and their conversation meandered from his duties at the fire station to her new job, which she enjoyed. She sipped water and when the French onion soup arrived, she savored the rich flavor, knowing she had so much to say.

"Uncle Fred would make a good theologian."

Clint's head popped up, leaving his soupspoon sloshing in midair. "Really. I've never pictured him in that light."

"No, but his answers are clear, and I'm really learning a lot about the meaning of faith. He's given me real-life examples, sort of like the parables Jesus used to answer questions, but he talks about things from his own life. It makes sense." She pressed her lips together, anxious to speak from her heart. "I'm understanding more each day, and I realize now I was never a true nonbeliever. I was more like a doubting Thomas. I needed to stick my fingers into…" She looked down at her soup and decided he didn't need the picture.

Clint grinned. "That's what I saw, Paula. I said you had the seeds, and I was right."

"I even understand the seeds now. You lost me with that analogy until I felt them growing in my—"

"Clint. How nice to see you."

Hearing a woman's syrupy voice, Paula lowered her spoon, the soup forgotten. She eyed the woman over her shoulder, seeing a head of blond hair sweeping to her shoulders, lashes longer than ones she'd seen on TV and flawless makeup. Confused, she shifted her attention back to Clint's face, pale as the napkin she'd laid on her lap.

"Elise. What are you doing here?"

While Paula recalled what Clint had told her about his former fiancée, Elise's laugh rippled above Paula's head.

"I'm having dinner. You seem to be doing the same."

He didn't speak but sought Paula's eyes with a look of apology. "This is an odd coincidence."

Irony seeped from Clint's tone, and from Elise's expression, Paula suspected his insinuation was correct.

"You knew I'd be here, didn't you?" This time his look could broil a steak.

"I didn't mean to interrupt." Elise eyed Clint with an arched brow, then snapped her eyes toward Paula. "I don't believe we've met."

Paula drew back, amazed that Elise had ignored Clint's question. Her pulse raced, anticipating where the conversation might lead.

"I doubt you've ever met." Clint's voice reeked with irritation. "Paula's only been in town a few months." He turned to her. "Paula, this is Elise Jordan, an old friend of mine. Elise, this is—"

The woman's laughter cut through the air.

"Friend?" She slipped behind him and rested her hand on his shoulder. "Interesting." She gave Paula a wink, then leaned down and kissed Clint's cheek.

He jerked away, his frown deep, his face blazing. "That's enough, Elise."

She drew back, her look as sharp as his voice. "I look forward to seeing you again, Clint…when you're in a better mood." She spun around, wiggling her fingers over her shoulder, and headed away from their table.

Clint released a ragged breath. "I'm sorry, Paula. That startled me. I know Elise wants what she wants, but this time she can't win." He shook his head. "Never."

Paula's lungs collapsed against her heart, and her head spun. Elise wanting what she wanted didn't have to be spoken. She'd seen it in the woman's determined expression. Even if she loved a man with all her heart and soul, she could never walk into an intimate situation such as this one and stake a claim so obvious it coiled around Paula like a snake.

Cobra came to mind.

She slid her soup aside, drew her salad closer but ignored it. Later she forced down two of the six perch fillets that were probably delicious. No matter what Clint said, his words rolled off her, and she drowned in uncertainty again. He'd shown his disgust, but the past had strength to undo the present. She'd almost allowed that to happen, and though

Clint had fortitude, Elise had been the woman he'd promised to marry years ago, and despite her embarrassing attempt to impact their date, she had only put a small dent in it. The woman had persistence. Viewing their past and Elise's determination, what guarantee did she have that Clint wouldn't think back and honor his past promise to Elise? She had beguiled him once. She could do it again.

Paula clung to her self-esteem, the faith beginning to settle in her heart and the image of her life with Clint, but it all seemed too good to be true. Somehow when her life held promise, reality dashed it to the ground.

What now? She could only pray to a God she'd rejected for so long, but a God she hoped loved her as He'd promised.

Devon had signaled to Clint before the morning meeting. He wanted something, but so did Clint, so he welcomed the opportunity. He settled into a chair, only half listening to the review of the past shift. Since the dinner Friday, his thoughts had dwelled on the coincidence of Elise showing up at Clawson Steak House.

Even though he'd been snide about the possibility, he'd worked it through in his head, and logic told him it had to be just that. A coincidence. But logic had a short life. The situation left him with the feeling she'd put one over on him. But how would she have known? No one knew about the date except Devon, which meant Ashley knew, but how Elise fit into the picture made no sense.

With that question hanging in his mind, Clint had wanted to ask Devon about the situation all day yesterday, but they'd been busy fighting a grass fire started by someone who knew burning trash was against the city ruling. The fire was followed by releasing a child whose head was stuck between the rungs of a staircase, and visiting the woman who fell and couldn't get up, which had become a weekly event since she loved the crew's visit and so did her dog. Loneliness was a sad situation. Something he'd learned from experience. Another fire blazed through much of the night, and he had been too tired to talk about anything.

Devon wound down the review, and the new lieutenant took over for the next crew's tasks and duties. When his part of the meeting ended, he rose and waited for Devon.

"Could I ask a favor?"

"Sure." Clint walked beside him to the locker room to change out of their uniforms.

Devon held the door. "My car's in the shop. Ashley dropped me off on Thursday, but she has the kids, and I hate to drag her into the cold. I told her I'd hitch a ride home. Do you mind?"

"No problem. I've been wanting to talk with you,

anyway." He stepped into his jeans and pulled a knit shirt over his head.

Devon had finished and sidled over to him while Clint put on his shoes. "What's up?"

Clint tied his sneaker and rose. "Have you run into Elise anywhere?"

"Elise? No." His face twisted to a scowl. "Why?"

"Somehow I think she knew I was taking Paula to the Clawson Steak House last Friday."

Devon's back straightened. "It wasn't me, and it wouldn't be Ash. We both know how you feel about that."

"I thought so, but someone must have said—"

"No. He wouldn't have." Devon's color heightened as his eyes narrowed. "If he did, I'll—"

"If who did?" Clint held his breath.

"Sal. He asked me the day you called her, and I didn't think a thing of it. You'd been talking about the gift card when he was there."

"But why would Sal—"

"Maureen used to be good friends with Elise."

Clint's hands rolled to fists. "If it was Sal, I'd have a few words for him, but Maureen's another story. I tell you, Dev, no matter who stirred up this trouble, I'm rabid."

Devon dropped his hand on Clint's shoulder. "I don't blame you."

Outside, a breeze swept through Clint's hair, and he sucked in the fresh air to rid him of the tainted smell of someone prying into his business. And he had no recourse. "Let's keep my life to ourselves from now on, Dev."

"Sorry. I didn't even think of Maureen until you asked."

He slapped Devon on the back. "I know you didn't mean anything, but you should have seen the show. I can't believe Elise would lower herself to groveling, but that's how it came across."

"She was always a manipulator, Clint. Love is blind. You never noticed, and I didn't plan to break the news. I figured one day you'd see it and take care of it yourself."

A puff of air shot from him as he wondered if he would have ever seen the truth. Elise was the first woman he'd thought he'd loved. If he'd experienced then what he had now, he would have known better.

Devon slipped into the passenger side, his thoughts seeming to be on the Elise situation. Having no interest in dragging it on, Clint changed the subject. The problem was one he had to resolve, and he could only hope Elise would lie low and realize she'd lost whatever she was after.

When he pulled into the driveway, Devon jumped out. "Come in. Ashley asked me to do a project, and I need a talented carpenter's advice." He gave Clint a wink.

"Happy to." Clint turned off the motor while Devon waited and then followed him to the house.

Devon opened the door, and footsteps pounded down the stairs. "Daddy." Kaylee opened her arms and clung to his legs while Joey charged behind and joined her. He crouched down and gave them both a big hug. "Tell your mom Clint's here to help me with the shelves she wants."

"Me, too." Joey pointed to his chest. "I can help."

Clint couldn't help but chuckle, and he scooted Joey into his arms. "Let's go, big man, and see what your mom has in mind."

"Shelves," Joey piped up, sweeping his arm toward the back of the house.

Clint gave him a squeeze, and as he came through the kitchen doorway, he skidded to a stop. "Paula. This is a nice surprise."

She gave a faint grin. He suspected her tinge of uncertainty resulted from the confrontation with Elise.

Ashley pointed toward the nook in the dining room. "I'd like to put some shelving in that wasted niche."

"Niche." Joey's voice split the air.

Everyone laughed, even Paula.

Ashley flagged the kids toward the living room while he and Devon studied the space, rather useless as he noted but shelving would add something useful. They tossed around ideas, measured and made some progress.

When he'd finished, he wandered back to the kitchen, hoping to join the conversation with Paula, but Joey tugged his arm and he followed him along with Kaylee into the living room.

The children had set up a toy village with a schoolhouse and playground, along with a school bus, and Kaylee seemed to be in charge of the house with pieces of furniture, little people and even a pet cat.

"Come, Clint." Joey beckoned him to sit. "You be the bus driver." He settled beside them, his long legs folded Indian fashion but too big to get close to the schoolhouse. When Joey rang the school bell, he rolled the bus forward, and Kaylee lifted a child from a chair and placed her in the bus. Joey took his turn, and soon he had a bus full, driving it across the carpet to the house. The children's laughter tickled him and he loved seeing their fun with the plastic village. One day... His chest tightened, imagining a day he would stand in a hospital and watch his child—his very own child—make his way into the world.

Prickles lifted on his skin, and he glanced over his shoulder to see Paula leaning against the doorjamb watching him.

"Having fun?" She ambled into the room, her focus on the children.

But seeing her expression, he sensed her mind was far away. More than once she'd indicated she would never be a mother, and her persistence took a chip out of his hope. He'd often told her she'd be a wonderful mother. He had no doubt she'd learned good attributes from living with a mother who'd lacked so much. He wished he could convince her to believe it.

Before he could hoist himself from the floor, she'd walked away, and his thoughts went with her. Helping Devon with the shelves reminded him that he'd nearly finished her storage unit. All he needed to add were the drawer pulls and hinges, and he couldn't wait to give it to her, but he needed to seek Ashley's help to find a way she could distract Paula so he could sneak it into the house.

As soon as the kids had lost interest in the village, he rose and headed for the kitchen, but instead he found Ashley and Paula in the dining room, involved in the final plans for Neely's baby shower. His plan to have a private moment with Ashley faded. He said his goodbyes and gave Paula a hug before he made his way outside, frustrated with Elise and the mess she'd made.

In the cold air, he had second thoughts. Maybe she'd done him a favor. If Paula didn't trust him enough to accept the truth, he needed to face it. He'd hoped to share his life with her, a life to outshine the old, but did he have it in him? Today he didn't know.

Still, no matter what happened between Paula and him, he had to stop Elise.

Neely waddled across the room and sank into the chair. Paula had opened a card table and piled her gifts nearby so she and Ashley had access. Recalling Neely's slender body when they came to Roscommon for her mother's funeral, today she looked more like Tweedledee or Tweedledum in Lewis Carroll's *Through the Looking-Glass*. Her round belly blocked her from getting close to the table.

"Great lunch. Loved that broccoli salad with bacon."

She thanked Neely's friend, whose name she'd already forgotten. She'd met too many people while trying to play hostess, something she'd never done in her life.

Ashley had bustled around, placing each guest's shower gift on the pile and steering her to the punch table. She remained in the kitchen organizing their menu of salads while the women gathered around the room, filling the sofa and chairs. Ashley had added folding chairs to the seating so they had just enough.

The room buzzed with sound. Women of all ages pointed to their gifts, seeming proud of the gigantic bows and appropriate adornments of pacifiers, rattles and stuffed animals hanging from the lids. When Ashley got their attention, the chattering stopped and the unwrapping began.

She handed Neely the gifts while Ashley added the type of present to the gift card so later Neely could send out thank-you notes. The whole tradition overwhelmed her as she realized she'd never attended a shower for any reason—wedding or baby. Her life had been sterile. She'd missed so much.

As she watched Neely display the gifts, her heart wrenched with envy. For years she'd set her mind to remain single despite Clint's differing argument. Yet today she had second thoughts. Maybe Clint made more sense than her warped viewpoint. Was it possible to take a negative and make it positive? Could the rotten experiences of her past make her even more determined to give her child a beautiful life filled with love, hope and even faith?

Though Elise's appearance in Clint's life had knocked her off her path, she'd dragged herself back onto her journey and reviewed the woman's aggressive behavior, her too-sure-of-herself attitude. Witnessing Clint's ex-fiancée's lack of tact, she'd finally recognized that Clint had looked at her with scorn not desire.

She knew him now. His heart spoke to her as much as words, and she'd allowed the envious woman, who'd either realized her mistake in letting him go or couldn't accept that she'd lost, to undo the foundation she and Clint had made in the months they'd known each other. They hadn't jumped into anything but inched along, each step bringing them closer together. She'd allowed herself to doubt the man she knew, in favor of a woman whose actions belied her confidence. Elise had lost her battle.

Yet whatever the woman had done, Paula recognized her behavior was worse. Her edginess with

Clint since Elise had ruined their dinner deserved an apology. If he didn't accept it, she would do whatever she had to do to rectify the damage. Fortifying her trust in Clint and the Lord still needed work, but apologizing to Clint would be a wise start.

Chapter Twelve

Clint slipped his credit card along the card reader and signed his name. With the bag in hand, he left the hardware store, anxious to get back to work on his project for Paula, since he still had a few things to finish.

His quick naps on the days he arrived home from his two-day shift had gotten to him. Being tired had become his middle name. Though he longed to see Paula, the storage unit of shelves and drawers was a housewarming gift. She'd moved in nearly two weeks ago.

The biggest surprise was she hadn't said a thing since the day she'd brought it up at her mother's house, but she still wanted something to fill a space in her living room between the staircase and the foyer, the perfect spot for it in size and purpose.

Feeling weariness overtake his enthusiasm, he eyed the coffee shop a few doors down. A mug of caffeine might help.

He unlocked the driver's door and tossed the sack holding hinges and drawer pulls into the passenger seat and locked the door. As he headed for the coffeehouse, he hoped he could get a couple of hours work done on the project before Paula wondered why he hadn't dropped by to see her this morning.

He stepped inside and stood in line as he read the posted menu. Settling for a plain mug of regular, he put in his order, paid the clerk and spun around to find a table. His heart skipped when he spotted Elise near the front window, and his intention faded. He turned toward the exit, preferring to drink the coffee in his car.

But before he acted on his plan, he had second thoughts. Maybe this meeting was meant to be. It offered him time to level with Elise and, as kind as he could be, put her in her place. But if he did, he would call Paula as soon as he finished. He'd learned his lesson. Then, using good sense, he forced his feet to retreat. It was too late. He heard her call his name, and a chill ran down his spine.

She beckoned, and he followed the wave of her hand, ignoring the knot in his stomach. This time he couldn't blame her for the meeting. "Elise." He eyed her overbright smile, wishing he'd acted on his first instinct. Run.

"How nice to see you." She motioned toward the seat beside her. Instead, he sat across from her, keeping his legs wrapped around the legs of his chair, fearing she might try to make foot contact. He didn't know what to expect from Elise anymore, and the concept of trust faded when he dealt with her.

"I'm pleased to see you." He grasped a napkin and wiped up the slosh from setting his cup on the table. "We need to talk and there's no time like the present."

"I agree." She leaned closer, glancing at the chair beside her.

"First, I know that Maureen told you I would be at the Clawson Steak House the night you ran into us."

Her head pulled back, and she opened her mouth as if to respond but closed it before she spoke.

"You don't need to make excuses. I'm just disappointed in you."

She lowered her eyes. "I made a bad decision. I'm sorry."

He ignored her apology. "You obviously see that I'm dating someone, but you need to understand that it's more than dating."

Her head lifted, inching upward as her eyes met his. "Really?" She gave him a coy look. "I've heard through the grapevine you hadn't dated for years since…" She added a teasing grin to the look. "So what caused the change?"

"Wisdom, and realizing I didn't care anymore."

Although she tried to cover her surprise, she failed. "Talking about grapevines, that sounds rather sour to me."

"No, Elise. You're wrong. It's a sweetness I've never experienced before."

This time, he'd struck an unwelcome chord. "With all your Christian upbringing, it appears you don't know how to forgive." A haughty expression gave her turned-up nose an extra tilt.

"No forgiveness needed."

Her eyes bored through him, piercing his spirit of kindness.

"But I would like to thank you. If you can remember, I have a strong feeling about marriage and what it means, and if I'd not been freed by your decision, I would have made one of the worst mistakes of my life."

She'd been vindictive with others but never with him, but today the stench of retribution sickened him. He'd approached their conversation without thinking about vengeance, and he could only wonder what she might do to get even. As far as he could see, the damage was done, but he needed to try.

He reached across the table and touched her hand, and though she recoiled, she reconsidered and wove her fingers through his. "You're trying to hurt me because I hurt you. Is that it?"

As he shifted his hand away from her grasp, he considered his responses and came up empty. "I never wanted to hurt you, Elise. That's not who I am. What I had wanted to do was understand what I lacked as a husband. What could I have done to change your mind? What you could have said to, at least, have given me a sense of closure rather than walking away. That's all I'd wanted."

Her bitter expression softened, and she looked down at their knotted fingers. "You've always had nice hands, Clint. Strong yet gentle. I'll always remember that." Her head inched upward until they were eye to eye. "What could you have done?" Her gaze drifted off into the distance. "Probably nothing. I became a pawn, I suppose you could call it. A trophy wife." Her eyes met his again. "Do you understand?"

He'd heard the term—a beautiful woman who strutted on the arm of her well-to-do husband, hosted his parties and did the right things to better his position with a company, and from it she gained money but little else. He nodded, feeling a pang of sadness for her. Elise had hit the pit of awareness. Even her self-esteem had reached bottom when she realized what she'd become. He observed it in her actions. She'd never been a groveler.

"It wasn't the life I wanted, Clint. The wife of a firefighter didn't hold much glamour, but the women knew their husbands would be home after their forty-eight-hour shifts, and while they'd been gone, they'd saved lives and property. Those women would never be rich, never wear glamorous attire and never live in a high-priced home, but they would have a different kind of security." Her eyes had misted.

His chest caved in, feeling a pang of regret, yet he knew better. Elise turned her emotions on and off like a light switch. "That's about it for the wife of a firefighter, except you missed something. His wife would have love and a best friend."

She looked away as if trying to hide the truth from his eyes. "And that's why I came back." Her head did a slow turn. "I messed up. I let a fairy-tale dream pull me from reality. I realized after a miserable two years I'd had the world in my hands... and I let you go."

His lungs emptied, and he swallowed air. He studied her face, trying to read the truth in her eyes, but he was as blinded as he'd been before she walked away.

Her fingers squeezed his. "Is there any hope, Clint? Even a speck will let me breathe."

Longing filled her face and smothered him, but as quickly as his heart melted, a warning signal screamed in his mind, and Paula's image covered the vision in front of him. He took a final gulp of coffee and rose. "Here's how it is, Elise, if I ever loved you, it's over, dead, gone. I want you to back off and let me live my life."

Though tears rolled down her cheeks, perseverance still sparked in her eyes. "But remember the beautiful times—"

"Elise, I don't make rash decisions. I'm thoughtful and take time to weigh what is right and good. I have new hopes that moved into the empty space you left. I don't have room for anyone else." He rose and grasped the chair back.

"I made a mistake, Clint. It was a—"

"You made two mistakes, Elise. Coming here was the other one. You're wasting your time in Ferndale." He slid the chair beneath the table. "I'm glad we had this talk. We both know where we stand."

He turned toward the door and didn't look back.

Clint pulled into Paula's driveway, his surprise for Paula loaded in the back of his neighbor's van. He would have been in a mess, trying to jam it in his trunk. He opened the van door and a northern wind, along with a few flakes of snow, sent an icy chill down his back. One thing Michigan always had was weather adventures. One day the temperature was sixty and the next it was twenty. He tucked his hands in his pockets before recalling the work gloves he'd slipped into the back.

Grateful that Devon had agreed to help him unload the cabinet, he opened the rear door and found the gloves. Today they would serve two purposes, and he appreciated the warmth.

He stood a moment and peered down the street. With no cars in sight, he slipped back inside the van to wait for him to arrive with the door key he'd gotten from Ashley. Not only had she volunteered the spare key Paula had given her in case of an emergency, she'd planned a girl's afternoon of shopping. They'd left early and he couldn't use the neighbor's van until he came back from a couple of errands so he suspected they would be back soon.

When he first met her, Paula hadn't been much of

a shopper that he'd noticed, but she'd come into her own the past months, and he loved the changes he'd seen. She'd become far more outgoing and confident. Though still persistent about taking it slow in their relationship until confident in her faith, she'd been more open with her affection. He'd even seen her playing with Ashley's kids, a smile blooming on her face bigger than theirs. That was what she needed—to prove to herself she could be a loving, nurturing mother.

Through the rearview mirror, he spotted Devon pulling up to the curb and he left the warmth of the van and closed the door.

Devon hurried from the car, his head wagging as if muddled. "Sorry, my dentist was running late, and it's icy out there, and I got held up by an accident."

"Anyone hurt?" Images slipped into his mind of so many times the department was called to accidents. Some tragic.

"Nothing serious, but it took them a while to clear traffic." Devon clapped his hands together. "Let's get this baby inside." He pulled work gloves from his jacket pocket, and they lowered the cabinet to the ground.

While Devon unlocked the door, Clint admired his handiwork, certain Paula would be overjoyed. The sheen shone in the daylight, and the intricate door panels gave him a sense of pride.

Devon darted back and lifted an end while Clint grasped the other, and they lugged it toward the front door. They maneuvered the stairs and then manipulated it through the doorway. Inside they lowered the cabinet and both blew out a stream of air.

Clint used his glove to wipe off the spots left by the melting snow. The clouds had looked gray and heavy, and he wished he'd had the brains to cover the wood with a tarp or painter's cloth in case of snow. The white flakes increasing by the second validated he was looking at the first heavy snowfall of the season.

"This is a beauty, Clint." Devon stood back and surveyed his creation, sliding his hand across the sheen and investigating the carved wood panels he'd designed. "Where does it go?"

Clint pointed to the space between the door and foyer, now empty except for a footstool that had become a catchall for coats, purses and mail. Devon hoisted his end, and together they shifted the cabinet close to the wall.

Clint stood back, eyeing the piece, and was satisfied. "That works, don't you think?"

Devon nodded. "Good spot. You couldn't find—"

His head shot up as did Clint's, hearing the back door open, and footsteps sounding in the kitchen.

"Devon? Is something wrong?" Paula came through the doorway and stumbled to a stop, snow leaving a trail on the carpet. She searched their faces while Clint's grin was about to burst open his cheeks. Then her eyes lowered. The packages slipped from her hands as she darted across the carpet and flung her arms around Clint's neck, her lips meeting his with such power he nearly lost his balance.

"I'd better leave and let you two enjoy the moment." Devon's chuckle faded as he passed through the dining room into the kitchen and out the door.

Though Clint wanted to thank Devon again for his help, he savored the moment, her kiss sweeter than the cotton candy he'd enjoyed as a kid. He could reiterate his thanks to Devon later.

She eased back, her cheeks warmed to pink, her eyes misted with pleasure. "You made this for me."

He could only nod, his lungs depleted from the kiss and the joy that tightened his throat.

"Clint, I can't believe you made this gorgeous cabinet for me." She leaned against his chest, her head, spotted with snowflakes, resting on his shoulder. Her heart beat in tune to his. "No one has ever—" Her head lifted and her eyes met his. "Enough of the past. I'm thrilled to the core."

Her hands slid down his arms as she turned and drew closer to the cabinet. "I love the wood. It's like dark honey and as shiny." She turned to face him. "And I can't believe these panels." She slipped off her coat and let it fall to the floor as she knelt and traced the lines of the curved design. She rose, shaking her head and pulling her coat from the floor. "This is more than I would have believed."

"That's because you're more than I can believe." He slipped his hand in hers. "I've been working on it since you said you admired mine, but then everything happened." He grinned, remembering what he'd gone through. "I wanted to work on it, but I wanted to see you so I was torn, and I had to squeeze it into free moments, and then the fire and hospital."

Her eyes met his again, and she tilted her lips to his. "But here it is." A glint sparked in her eyes. "And here we are."

The meaning enveloped him, and he drew her closer, sensing everything would be all right.

She drew in a deep breath, but her smile remained. "I've been thinking, and..." She looked toward the seating arrangement. "Let's sit."

He wove his fingers through hers and followed her to the sofa. She pressed her back into the corner facing him while he sat on the edge of the cushion convincing himself she had good news. Eager to feel at ease, he opened his mouth to ask, but he cautioned himself. Letting her begin at her own speed was something he had to learn. Firefighters got down to business, needing facts and resolution. He'd learned Paula didn't work that way.

She gave him a tender look. "Relax."

Her soft voice accompanied her fingers squeezing his. He scooted back and rested his body against the sofa.

"I've given you a rough time, Clint. I never meant to, but as you know trusting someone fell in line with locking myself in a cage with a tiger."

Her eyes shifted away from him, and his chest contracted against his lungs.

"The tiger is gone. So is the cage. I trust you more than anyone." Her gaze met his. "I know that leaves a question, but I'm not worried about it. I see changes every day. I'm open to learning to live a life I've never lived, and I have you to thank. You and my uncle and cousins, but most of all you."

He searched her face for the direction she was headed. "Why are you thanking me?" Tension struck his spine, forcing him to shift his body and his mind to pleasant thoughts.

"Because you eased me out of hiding. You made me comfortable enough to tell about things I'd hidden for years, even hid them from myself. The words spilled out little by little, Clint, and instead of making judgment, you accepted me for who I am today."

He'd done that although he'd worked at it in those moments when he questioned her ability to stay in the new life she'd found. Old habits creep out with no warning like garbage in a drain. But no plumber could solve the problem. Only trust and faith.

A frown hinted at the corner of her mouth. "You're still worried."

"Not anymore."

"I'm not, either. You know I grappled with Elise's appearance in town although I tried to convince myself it meant nothing. I'm still bad at that but I'm getting better."

"I see the change."

A grin replaced her frown. "You see things before they're evident to me, Clint. I wish I could do that."

"One day you will when—"

"When we've known each other for years."

His heart pitched. "Are you telling me you want to—"

"Yes. I want to move forward with us. We have a solid friendship, but I've never allowed our relationship to go beyond that, never believed it could lead to commitment even though part of me wanted it." Her eyes searched his. "But I'm ready. More than ready."

Tension fell away as relief and happiness took its place. He rose and drew her up, his mouth touching hers, tender at first until he could no longer hold back the feelings bursting inside him.

Paula softened in his arms, her fingers exploring his hair, her lips eager and warm on his, and they clung together until their bound emotions released into pure joy. She drew back, her eyes glowing, and her face filled with a profound meaning he understood.

Recognizing the danger of their zeal, he rocked back and viewed her at arm's length, admiring her whole being, a beautiful creation he wanted to hold forever.

In their calm, they settled again on the sofa. Paula thanked him again for his handiwork and for his part in helping her find herself. He had her to thank, too, and he expressed his own gratefulness. "When you reminded me that the problems between Elise and me might not have anything to do with my faults or weaknesses, I began to think for the first time. I reviewed the issues that seemed small at the time and understood how those could grow and be a wedge between us. I suppose that's why finding someone who shared my values and faith was important."

"I understood that, Clint. But what about Elise's beliefs? Her behavior seems to go against that in some ways."

He nodded, having been startled by Elise crawling to him and begging. He'd never witnessed that weakness in her, but then he'd put her on a pedestal. She'd been the first beautiful woman who'd shown him so much attention. "We all have twisted perceptions at times. I sure had mine. I recognized her manipulation in certain situation, but she laid on the flattery that I fell for, never having experienced it, and I thought it was exciting."

"Many women know how to beguile. Some of us don't."

"What?" He couldn't help but chuckle. "You beguiled me, but then I'm easy."

"No. Not anymore. You know what you want, and you speak your mind. I loved that in you."

"And what about Elise? Are you comfortable with how it's been resolved?"

She only looked at him, and he knew she wasn't.

"What do you think? I've told you everything."

"You did, and I felt good because it meant you trusted me." She paused a moment before she continued. "I know this will sound silly, but I'd like to talk with her."

His head flew back, startled by her idea. "Why? What good would it do?"

She shrugged. "I don't know for sure, but I feel something telling me that I should. In some ways, I see similarities between us. A kind of desperation and hunger for being loved. I guess I'd like to give her hope."

She'd knocked the wind out of him. "Are you telling me you feel sorry for her?"

Her eyes became thoughtful. "I suppose you could call it that." She shook her head. "I realize it's not going to happen, but it's a strong feeling I have. It's sort of…a sign of forgiveness."

The weight of her desire pinned him to the spot. The idea of forgiveness made good sense, but he wasn't sure. He closed his eyes, massaging the center of his forehead, seeking the answer to what was right or wrong. What did she hope to accomplish if Elise balked? Paula could be hurt by Elise's sharp tongue, or… He ran out of steam but knew he had to do what was right. "I have her cell phone number." He captured her gaze. "Do you want it?"

She studied him a moment as if surprised that he'd offered. Finally she nodded. "If you don't mind.

I'll give it more thought before I act on this feeling, but I sense it's the right thing to do."

Trust meant standing by her decision, and he would. He hit the call log in his cell phone and jotted down her number. When he handed it to her, she didn't look at it. She clutched it in her hand and looked at him. "Thank you for having faith in me."

"I've had that for a long time."

She rose and crossed the room, brushing her hand along the cabinet. "I know you have." Her head turned to look at him over her shoulder. "Did you notice how much it's snowed?"

He gazed through the window, watching white flakes drift past on the wind, streaks of white mounding on the window ledge, and he rose to stand beside her.

She slid her arm around his waist. "Let's do something fun."

Surprised, he shifted to face her. "Okay. What did you have in mind?"

"Let's see if Neely would let us take all the kids to the park. She's in no condition to slip around outside and play with them, and look." She pointed to the pristine landscape. "They'll love it."

Amazed, his eyes shot heavenward, and he drew her into his embrace and spun her around. "Now that is fun. Let's call Neely."

Chapter Thirteen

Before Clint could open his car door, Joey and Kaylee barreled out of the backseat. He pressed the handle and darted out into the slippery snow. "Wait up, you urchins."

Kaylee slid to a stop. "We're not urchins."

Paula swung open her door and stepped outside, not waiting for him to be the gentleman he liked to be. He grinned, realizing he'd probably have to get used to it.

But she appeared to have a mission. "Ready for the slides?" She plowed through the snow and reached them.

Clint gazed at the white mound and scooped a handful into his gloves. The flakes formed into a soft ball, and he chuckled as he gave it a toss, and it hit Paula in the back.

Laughing, she swung around. "No, you don't." She beckoned to the children, and in moments, they were forming their own weapons, and he ducked as the missiles sailed past him except for the one that hit him in the chest. Surprised, he chuckled, seeing the snowball hitting the mark belonged to Joey.

In playful retribution, he grabbed another glob, packed it and tossed it the boy's way. It hit his arm, and in his eagerness to dodge it, he slipped and landed in a fluffy blanket of snow.

When Paula saw him on the ground, her enthusiasm grew. She skittered around and found a nearby pristine patch of snow and fell over backward, flailing her arms and legs, creating a snow angel.

Joey tugged his jacket and dragged him forward. "Make a boy one, Uncle Clint."

The uncle reference swelled in his heart. Though he wasn't the boy's uncle, the title caused images to grow in his mind of Paula and him playing in the white landscape with their own son or daughter. He gave Joey a thumbs-up and selected a spot near Paula's and followed her method, flinging himself into the icy snow, some slipping beneath his collar, and waved his arms and legs to create another angel.

In moments, Kaylee mimicked him, followed by Joey, who added his imprint to the landscape. Their laughter echoed in the cloud-heavy sky, and though an icy stream rolled from his neck down his back, he warmed at the joy of seeing Paula with the children.

Her cheeks rosy and eyes glowing, Paula sidled beside him, and he reached out with one arm for an embrace when he realized her motivation wasn't romantic. Her arm stretched out, but instead of accepting his hug, she slipped a glob of snow down his neck, the icy mush sending a chill down his chest.

Wet and laughing, she fell into his arms while the children giggled and darted to them, their arms wrapped around their bodies as high as they could reach. They joined hands and swung in a circle until his foot slipped and they piled onto the ground in a giggling bundle of jackets, boots and happiness.

"You're going to freeze to death with that wet mess up your sleeves." Paula crouched in front of Kaylee, brushing the snow from her clothing and checking beneath for icy particles.

"Not me." Kaylee spun away. "Let's swing."

With piping voices, Joey and Kaylee bounded to the playground while Clint slipped his fingers through Paula's and followed them. He eyed her bright smile, the sunlight glowing on her face, and the cold from the snow vanished. "Having fun?"

Her face gave the answer. "The most I've had in years." Her eyes searched his. "Maybe a lifetime."

He squeezed her hand, wanting to see her as happy every day of her life. "I forgot how much fun it is to be a child."

"And how much fun to play with them." A telling look wove through his body. "I've told you so often being a mother is a natural instinct that comes from being content and loving them and yourself."

"And their father."

A lump formed in his throat and speaking seemed

impossible. He slowed and planted a kiss on her forehead. "Thank you."

"I've been a determined woman despite my lack of so many things, but somewhere along the line, I knew what was right. I just had to dig deep to find it." Her hand left his and slipped behind him. "I thank you for that."

The step she'd taken was more than he had asked for. He'd expected to romp in the snow with the kids and let them enjoy the first snow, but Paula had fired his dreams. They'd made the first step in creating a lasting relationship, and today she'd added the element he'd longed for his entire adult life. A child of his own.

Paula stood outside the coffee shop, pondering the wisdom of her phone call to Elise. She heard an attitude in her voice, and she anticipated the worst until she reviewed why she'd called, and the sense of need that hung in her mind. Her need or Elise's? That was yet to be seen. A chill shivered down her back, and she braced herself and tugged open the café door, fighting the wind that had crept up since she'd left the house.

Hoping she remembered what Elise looked like, she scanned the customers and spotted her in a back booth. Before heading toward her, she ordered a mocha latte and added "skinny" to the description. Low-fat milk helped relieve the guilt of indulging in the rich treat. She waited, her eyes glued to the barista rather than connecting with Elise's gaze.

Struggling with second thoughts, she dug into her bag for her cash, and when she paid for the mug, she noticed the white heart-shaped design floating on the chocolate drink, and her own heart softened. She'd been motivated by sadness for the woman's inability to face the truth and the future, a situation she'd taken too long to handle. Not knowing what would happen, Paula turned and headed for her table.

Elise's eyes followed her across the room, an unpleasant look carved into her face, and all Paula could muster was regret for her own misjudgments and mistakes. She managed to frame a noncommittal expression on her face and approach her.

"Elise, thanks for seeing me." She set her drink on the table and scooted into the booth. "The last time we met was under a tense situation, and—"

"Do you think this is a tea party?" Elise's eyes snapped as fiery as her question.

"No, but it's also not to argue. There is none from my viewpoint."

Though Elise's response was a snort, her ramrod spine bent almost imperceptibly.

Using one of her mother's outdated phrases, she'd knocked the starch from her, but that hadn't been her purpose. She gave Elise a direct look. "I'm not here to cause trouble or to flaunt myself as a winner, and I'm sorry if that's what you thought."

Elise leaned forward, her voice a hiss. "I don't know why I agreed to seeing you. Curiosity, I suppose, trying to figure out what Clint sees in you. I'm still lost."

Without knowing, Elise had introduced the heart of the matter. "I know you're lost. I was lost once, too."

Her haughty look morphed to a look of confusion. "I have no idea what you mean."

Instead of wasting time with trying to make her understand, Paula began her story. The family background, what happened, and then she came to the why. "Since meeting Clint and beginning to feel better about myself, I faced a truth about me. I wanted love so badly I would do anything to get it. So hungry for it that I closed my eyes to morals and values, and I opened myself to diminished self-esteem that was already feeble. I'm grateful that I dug my way out of the pit."

Although Elise tried to hide her interest, she let the truth slip. "I'm not in a pit. I'm—"

"You may define pit differently. To me, it's fooling myself to believe that others did this to me, that I was the innocent party in a horrible plot." She closed her eyes, fighting back tears. "So I created a plot of my own. For me it was a perfect family, a mother and father who adored me and stood behind me even in my poor judgments. Like a novel, a subplot entered the picture. But this one wasn't from my imagination, it was from my life. I had the idea that true love, romantic love, could happen if I gave my all, if I paid for it in some way."

She looked into Elise's eyes, wanting to stress her point. "Your plot is perhaps opposite. Maybe you really did come from a perfect family."

"It doesn't matter what kind of family, and it's not your business." She'd risen on her haunches again.

"It's only your business, but analyze it. Sometimes families not only stand behind us but they shower us with so much we begin to think they owe us. I'm sure you know someone like that."

Discomfort spread across Elise's face, and Paula knew she'd hit the mark. "The problem is parents love their children because they're an extension of themselves. Some resent their children for the same reason." Her expression grew questioning.

"My mother didn't need a child in her shaky relationship. My father split when I was a toddler as far as I know. I'd never met him, and my mother, I suspect, unconsciously blamed me both for the marriage and the lack of love and support. The same thing I sought as an adult."

Elise's questioning expression remained unchanged, and her attention grew as she listened. "I had a good family. I don't see anything wrong with wanting the same."

"I'd want the same, too, but I didn't have that." Paula gave her a pointed look. "And you had a man who offered you that same kind of love and happiness, but you decided that wasn't as important as another image you had."

"What image are you talking about?"

Paula shrugged. "You have to answer that. Wealth, adventure, glamour, position, all of the above. Somewhere along the line, Elise, you forgot to value partnership to build a marriage, companionship, security or faithfulness to a man who adored you. How did you lose that?"

Elise closed her eyes and turned away.

Facing the truth took time and Paula sat back, waiting to see if Elise would walk out on her or be willing to learn.

"I believed in a fairy tale." Her voice was a whisper.

Paula nodded, remembering each time her fairy tale crashed to the ground. "I wanted that, too, and to your loss, I found mine. I'm not here to rub it in or chastise you for your blatant behavior with Clint. He doesn't feel that way. He only felt uneasy and sad."

"Sad?"

"He has a good heart, and though firefighters have a strong, capable reputation, they're also sensitive and kind. If you only knew what he put up with until recently, you'd understand me. He didn't give up on me. He persisted. He saw my hurt and my lack of faith in anything, and he served as an example of what life can be if we open ourselves to it. Love takes work and fortitude. That's one way it differs from the fairy tale." Her mind flashed back from her first meeting with Clint, her struggle to stay aloof, her failure to remain that way and yet the determination to back away.

"My parents didn't seem to work at their marriage." Elise's frown deepened. "I never saw them disagree or argue."

"They never allowed you to see it. Some people handle their issues in private, wanting their children to only see a happy home. Perfection is another fairy tale. No matter how hard we try, we can't always cut it."

She nodded, staring at the tabletop as if digging back in time to locate the clues.

"I was like elastic with Clint, or a pendulum, swinging madly in one direction and then catapulting in the other. He's one of the most patient people I know. If you'd given him time, you may have learned to understand him and see the beauty of him."

Shaking her head, Elise brushed a tear from her cheek. "He deserves you, Paula."

Paula's body jerked with the sting of her statement.

Elise's expression softened, a faint grin curving her lips. "I mean that in a good way. I would never have been good for him. Maybe one of these days I'll see what you're seeing, but I think I knew from the moment I accepted the ring that I'd made a bad move."

"Then why did you—"

"Come back?"

Paula nodded.

She shrugged. "I don't know. Somehow I thought he'd be better than nothing. You're right that he's kind and thoughtful. Sometimes it drove me crazy. I wanted spice and I got sugar. Know what I mean?"

Though Paula understood the analogy, she didn't comprehend her way of thinking. "Then you really did him a huge favor by saying goodbye. He's said that to me, but I wasn't as confident as he was." Opening her heart and thoughts to Elise began to take a toll. Her knee had begun to bounce, and her mind tripped over the thoughts she'd shared and the emotion she'd shown. "I wasn't confident then, but I am now."

Inching her head upward, Elise's eyes caught hers. "This is strange coming from me, but thank you."

The apology left her speechless. She swallowed with no avail, her throat locked with astonishment. "Thank you. I hope you find someone who'll be perfect for you."

Elise shrugged again. "Perfect isn't possible, but that would be nice. Maybe I will one day, but you're right. I can't make it happen. I can only leave the door open."

Grateful for the words that filled her heart and mind, Paula nodded.

"Would you say goodbye to Clint for me? I think I'll head back to the big city. I know one thing about myself. I'm not a small-town girl. I like a little excitement."

Paula grinned and promised she would relay her goodbye to Clint, but as Elise rose and headed for the door, she chuckled. She liked a little excitement, too, and she'd found all the excitement she could handle right there in Clint's arms.

Clint leaned back in Paula's easy chair, relieved when he listened to the full story of her talk with Elise. "You think it went well."

"Not at first. When I walked in she had an attitude, but I suppose I did, too. I arched my back like an angry cat."

He scowled, not certain he understood. "Then how did—"

"I was wrong. As I talked to her, I began to feel pity again. Can you believe it?" She bit her lip and closed her eyes. "I was right about seeing some of my problems in her, Clint." She drew in a lengthy breath. "And not a good me, but one who let her self-esteem sink while she begged for attention, begged someone to love her."

Emotions coiled in his chest, recalling Elise almost begging for his love. It was a side of Elise he'd never seen.

Paula straightened her back. "The good news is it ended well. She listened, and I think she understood."

"I suspect she did. You had nothing to gain by

talking with her unless you'd gone there to gloat, and I know that's not what you did."

She looked away. "Gloating would have been easier than offering advice, but that's what I did." Her head turned his way and she smacked her hands together. "So let's cheer up and talk about something more pleasant."

"Great idea." She offered the perfect lead-in for what he hoped she would welcome, but with Paula he never knew. "My folks are coming to visit next weekend."

She looked at him as if waiting for more.

"It's Thanksgiving, and they're anxious to meet you."

Tension returned to Paula's face, and he looked away and focused on the cabinet he'd built for her. He waited a moment, hoping she'd say something, but she didn't. "What do you think?"

Paula stared at him, as if trying to digest his simple request. "You know how I am about meeting people I don't know."

"I've told Mom and Dad about you, and naturally they're curious. I thought it was time you should be introduced." He tried to understand her hesitation. She'd never had parents like his, and maybe she worried it would bother her.

She looked more thoughtful. "For Thanksgiving, you said?"

He nodded.

"The dinner will be at your house, I hope."

"The dinner. Yes." He swallowed, wishing she were more excited. "And it's my birthday, too. This year it's the day after Thanksgiving."

He watched her shoulders ease, and finally she grinned. "You're still admitting you have birthdays? I gave that up when I turned thirty." Her grin broadened. "We'll have to do something special to celebrate. How about if I bring the birthday cake?"

Seeing her enthusiasm change, he told her the second part of his plan. "Since you want to do something special for my birthday, I thought you would like to host the birthday party. You don't have to fuss. Maybe we'll have pie left from Thanksgiving and—"

"You should have a cake, but I'm not much of a baker." She rolled her eyes. "But I spotted a place that sells cakes for all occasions. Much better than I could make, I'm sure."

"It's probably the same place I get them." Although he didn't want to admit he'd told his parents how much she meant to him, he rested his hand on her shoulder, admitting the rest. "My first motive is letting them see your new house, and the second is I want them to take a look at my latest handiwork."

She turned toward the cabinet he'd made for her and nodded. "You should be proud. It's beautiful." She shifted closer to him and touched his cheek.

Contentment eased through him.

"But here's my problem."

The *but* jarred the warm moment.

"I'll serve dessert, but if you want them to visit here, it means I need to do something festive with the house. A wreath, at least, or something."

Though his parents wouldn't expect decorations, he knew Paula, and he was glad this was motivating her. She'd already hinted not to expect her to put up Christmas decorations, and if his parents' visit motivated her, then he would give her an extra push. With no family traditions in her life, he longed to see that change now that he hoped to be part of her future. He slid up his sleeve and peered at his watch, an idea brewing. "What are you doing now?"

"Talking with you." She patted his shoulder, a crooked smile on her face. "I'm not busy, but why are you asking?"

"If you have no plans, then let's go." Before she asked what he meant, he reached for his jacket, slipped it on and pulled up the zipper.

"Go?" Her expression shifted from uncertainty to understanding. "You mean shopping for a wreath?" She shook her head. "I can do that on my way home from work."

"But can you purchase a tree?"

Her eyebrows arched high above her eyes. "You mean Christmas tree? But I told you I don't do decorations. Anyway it's too early for that?"

"Maybe you didn't do it in your old life, but this is your new one, remember?" He managed a playful grin. "Anyway, we have to put up two." He pointed to her and then pressed his index finger into his chest. "Yours and mine."

"But that means ornaments. I don't own any. I left behind all the scraggily ones my mother had packed in a box for years and tossed into storage unprotected. She never put up a tree. I saw them when I was packing—covered in dust, chipped and broken." She lowered her eyes. "And they reminded me of the way my life had been until I moved here." She raised her chin, her eyes meeting his. "And before I met you."

He shifted closer and wrapped her in his arms. His pulse raced, seeing the look on her face. "I want this Christmas to be a reflection of us—the happy us."

Tension melted from her body as a new look washed across her face. "Okay, it is our first Christmas together." She lifted her index finger and shook it at him. "But decorating's your baby, not mine."

His arms slipped from their embrace, and he pulled gloves from his pocket, a soft chuckle as he thought of a comeback. "My baby? It takes two for that."

She only shook her head and grinned.

His hope rose for their commitment to marry, and the thought of having their own child became closer to a reality, but before anything went wrong with his plan today, he pulled her coat from the foyer closet and held it out for her.

She slipped into it and wound a scarf around her neck with no comments.

He hoped her thoughts were the same as his, envisioning what their life could be like together.

Chapter Fourteen

Paula opened her front door. The wreath she'd purchased, adorned with pine cones and red berries, looked appropriate for both Thanksgiving and Christmas.

Clint stood on the welcome mat with a large bag in his hand with a logo she couldn't see. "That looks nice." He gestured to the door decoration and stomped his feet to remove the snow.

"Thanks." She smiled, wishing they could do more than stay home while she baked and he set up the tree.

Clint stepped inside and gave her a fleeting kiss, his lips and cheeks cold from the icy wind. "Here." He held out the sack, a grin lighting his face, and then he slipped off his jacket and hung it in the closet.

Holding it, she was able to read the logo. "What were you doing there?" She held up the sack, curious what was inside.

"I had to stop in Royal Oak, and I dropped in to Shine Gift Shop just to look, but I picked up something." He strode past her into the living room. "Take a look."

She opened the top and peered inside. "More Christmas balls." Curious, she lifted the container and admired the amazing handblown balls with Jesus in the manger inside. "These are gorgeous."

"I'd hoped you'd like them." She did love them, but she couldn't help but shake her head.

She'd tried to convince him she'd planned to be low-key this Christmas with so much going on, but she didn't say any more, not after the lovely gift.

When they went shopping she'd worked to convince him she only wanted an artificial slimline tree. Thinking back, she grinned. Clint had squinted at her as if he couldn't understand. "But it's not real. What about the smell of pine?"

"But think of the advantages," she had said as they stood in front of the five-foot tree. "They look real, and I won't have to deal with falling needles and sticky sap." She could see she hadn't convinced him yet, but then she became inspired and had more ammunition. "And being a firefighter, you know the possibility of tree fires, especially with the tree going up early. I won't have to worry about it."

She chuckled when his brow unfurrowed. "You're right," he'd said. "That's a good point." In the months they'd been together, she'd learned how to reason with a firefighter.

"Why the silly grin on your face?" He gave her a sidelong look.

"Thinking about our differences of opinion on decorating for the holidays."

He drew her into his arms. "But we're talking about Christmas."

She wiggled from his arms, knowing if she stayed she'd forget everything she had to do tonight. "Tomorrow's Thanksgiving and I'll be busy getting the house ready for your parents' visit on your birthday, so if you want to set up that tree tonight, you'll have to do it alone."

"But what about listening to Christmas music and drinking hot chocolate?" He gave her a playful pout, and she had to laugh. She'd never seen him look so boyish.

"Another year." She raised her finger and tapped his chest. "Or after your parents' visit. All this stuff can wait."

He lifted his shoulders, and his breath released in a narrow stream. "I can do it myself. It's a small tree." He gave her a pointed look as if reminding her she was the one who insisted on a slimline tree. "You go and make your cookies or whatever you're making."

Feeling as if she was deserting him, she headed into the kitchen to make his birthday cake, not cookies. She had a recipe that sounded good and it looked fairly easy.

While she pulled out the bowls and measuring cups, she thought back to when they were in the checkout line. Clint made her grin with his exuberance, but what surprised her was when he pulled out his wallet. She'd tried to stop him. "This is my tree and decorations, Clint, not yours. I should pay for it." But he'd insisted.

The clerk did a double take. "I've never experienced a married couple with separate accounts." She chuckled. "Not a bad idea."

She'd opened her mouth to correct the woman, but Clint gave her a subtle look, wanting her to let it go. She'd been confused by his reaction, but she'd let it slip. Now the question rose again.

She set down the poppy seeds and walked back into the living room.

Clint was on the floor tightening the screws of the tree stand while trying to hold the tree straight. She chuckled. "It looks like the leaning tower of Christmas." She hurried to his rescue.

He gazed up at her. "Is it crooked?"

"A little." She pressed her lips together not to laugh, but he'd looked so surprised she couldn't disillusion him.

He adjusted the tree and finished before he rose and stood beside her. They stepped back and agreed they'd done a good job.

Slipping his arm around her, Clint drew her closer. "What happened to the cookies?"

She'd wanted to surprise him with a birthday cake, and he wasn't making it easy.

"A question popped into my head and I got distracted."

He eyed her a minute. "Okay. Shoot."

"Why didn't you correct the clerk when she thought we were married?" Her mind whirled with possibilities of what his answer might be.

"No reason, but it sounded nice, don't you think?" He pulled open the bag with the Christmas paraphernalia they purchased together.

She gave him a poke. "But it's a lie. You don't believe in lying."

He shrugged. "Not exactly."

She gazed at him, weighing his meaning. She'd agreed to see where things would go, but the idea of marriage becoming a possibility still seemed unreal. Yet as she studied his strong profile, she couldn't image life without him.

"Shoo." Clint whisked her away toward the kitchen. "You're baking and I'm hanging lights." He grinned at her. "I can do the lights by myself." He gave her a wink. "And you know I don't lie."

Her breath drained as she gazed at him, so much a part of her life already, and yet reservations still blocked her ability to tell him the final degradation that she'd been unable to dump at his feet. The Lord knew everything and had forgiven her, but Clint didn't know, and she feared her admission would be the final blow that would destroy what could be a beautiful ending to her sad life. She sensed he loved her, knew it in her heart, but his human nature could see her confession as a threat to their future. The thought sickened her.

Though weighted by the thought, she pulled her shoulders back and marched into the kitchen while Clint wound the tree with lights. She needed the Lord's light in her life, but she wanted Clint's shining face in her world, too. He made everything worthwhile, and she wished she would have told him everything earlier when she'd found the courage to spill it out weeks ago.

But tomorrow his parents would visit for Thanksgiving, and on Friday they would celebrate his birthday. Now wasn't the time to ruin a lovely day. She buried the sorrow inside her as she'd done so much in her life and sought a smile as she added the ingredients to the poppy-seed cake, hoping it tasted as good as it sounded. Most of all she wanted Clint and his parents to enjoy it.

"Paula, this has been lovely meeting you, and the cake was scrumptious. I've seen poppy-seed muffins but never a cake. You'll have to give me the recipe."

"I'd be happy to." Paula grinned at the petite woman who was half the size of Clint or her husband. "Did you see the amazing cabinet Clint made for me as a housewarming gift?" She motioned toward the living room archway.

"Yes, I did. It's lovely. He's always tinkered with wood even as a boy." Pride shone in her eyes.

Paula loved seeing her response. "I'm sure you're proud of him."

"Aren't all parents?" She flashed Clint a smile, but beneath his pleasant nod, Paula recognized a grimace, and she knew it was for her. "Tell us about your parents. I'm sure we'll meet them one—"

"Mom." Clint's voice halted her, and she looked at him with a scowl. "I thought I mentioned Paula's mother died recently."

She slammed her hand over her mouth. "I'm so sorry. I—"

"It's perfectly all right, Mrs. Donatelli. I know—"

"Goodness, thank you, dear, and please, call me Iris." She gestured toward Clint's father. "And Clint's dad is Tony."

He smiled and nodded. "It's not like we're strangers. We've heard so much about you. In fact, we bugged Clint for weeks to bring you for a visit, but he explained you were getting settled in this lovely house." He glanced at Clint. "Although I'll never understand—"

"Dad." Clint's voice shot out a near bark. "Sorry." He shook his head and looked chagrined. "I didn't mean to sound so vehement, but let's talk about something else."

Seeing his discomfort and guessing what his father had nearly said, Paula came to Clint's rescue. "Tell me about Clint when he was a boy."

His father chuckled. "Now that will be fun." He flashed a look at Clint and began a tale about Clint learning to play catch as a boy.

Paula leaned back, relaxed for the first time since they'd arrived. Although they were lovely people, she couldn't stop thinking about her difficult confession. They needed to end their relationship or embrace it, and she couldn't until she opened up even more than she had.

The stories led through his first crush on his fourth-grade teacher, and later his dating in high school and the proms. She noticed in all their stories, some funny and some touching, they skirted the issue of Elise. That made her respect them even more. Her own mother wouldn't have hidden much of anything that she could pin on her.

As the thought landed in her mind, she swept it away. She'd asked the Lord for forgiveness and it was time she learned to forgive her mother. Nodding in response to Clint's youthful antics, she reviewed her mother's difficult life.

Left with a toddler, her mother had managed to keep her fed and clothed. Though she'd been close-mouthed about Paula's father, she'd spoken a bit about her past and much more as she drew near to death. No wonder life had been a horrible memory for her. As she dug deeper into her mother's trials, a quiet filled her, and for the first time, she had an understanding of how her mother had been raised, along with the horrors of her past, especially her uncle's sexual abuse, and forgiveness seemed unnecessary. The anger and hurt Paula had felt for so long shrank to a lump as small as an acorn.

When she cleared her mind, Clint was looking at her, concern growing on his face, and his mother's story had slowed—probably noting her withdrawal from their tales.

She grasped the only reasonable response she had. "Sorry. I remembered the gift I have for Clint. I haven't given it to him yet."

His mother clapped her hands. "Yes. Thank you for reminding me. I would have forgotten, too." She bent over, grasped her purse handle and pulled it into her lap. "We never know what to get this man." She chuckled. "He has everything, I think."

"I know. I had the same problem." Paula rose. "Excuse me a moment." She darted up the stairs and returned with a large wrapped package. All eyes turned her way as she walked into the room and handed Clint the gift. He gave it a questioning look. "This is big."

She only nodded. "Open your parents' first."

He slid open the envelope flap and pulled out a card, read it and raised his head. "Thank you for the message, and for the wonderful gift certificate. You were too generous."

His dad grinned. "Buy something you need, son. As your mother said, we're at a loss."

Clint rose and shook his father's hand, then

leaned down to give him a quick hug before moving to his mother and kissing her cheek.

Paula saw the love he had for his parents, the kind of family she'd longed for, and seeing them warmed her.

Clint returned to his chair and lifted her package. He read the card, a smile growing on his face, and then tore back the paper and pried up the box lid. When he pulled it back, he glanced at her, his expression a blend of surprise and happiness. "This is great."

She knew he spotted the stable roof projecting from the bottom of the box.

He reached inside and pulled out two figures wrapped in bubble wrap. He pulled it off the first, revealing a shepherd, and the second, Mary seated on a bed of hay.

His mother rose and peeked in the box. "This is wonderful. Tony, it's a crèche."

"A what?" His father stood up and craned his neck toward the box. "What in the world—"

"A nativity scene, Dad, for Christmas." Clint gave a laugh and winked at Paula.

Although Paula smiled, she'd drawn a blank. "I'm with you, Tony."

He shifted to her side and slipped his arm around her. "Now this is my kind of woman. Honest and pretty as a picture." His arm slipped away and he settled back into the chair.

Though a little embarrassed, she was drawn to

his Italian charm so like Clint at times. "Thanks. You're too kind."

"Not one bit," his mother said. "Our son has good taste…most of the time." She arched an eyebrow, and her action spoke a thousand words. Maybe Elise hadn't impressed them as much as she had Clint. Her curiosity rose, and she longed to ask his mother, but she tethered the idea.

She and Iris joined Clint in unwrapping the shepherds, sheep, camel, cow, three Wise Men, Joseph and finally the baby Jesus in the manger. The Holy Family sat in no particular order beside the stable.

"The details are beautiful. It looks Italian. Don't you think, Tony?" She held up one of the shepherds.

Before he could respond, Paula answered. "It's a Fontanini design from Italy. I fell in love with them when Clint and I were in Frankenmuth, and—"

"But you didn't buy it then." Clint's voice rang with surprise.

"No. I ordered it online." She warmed at his amazement that she'd done that for him. "You're worth it."

He rose and drew her into his arms. "I love it, Paula." His eyes probed hers. "It means so much to me."

She understood, and the devotion she'd felt in viewing the nativity scene filled her heart.

Tony stood. "Since we're all standing, I think we should get moving. We have a long drive home, and evening always means slippery weather."

Iris joined him, and while Clint pulled their coats from the foyer closet, they gave her hugs and compliments on the birthday cake. She'd forgotten to copy the recipe so she promised to send it. After more hugs, Clint walked them to the car while she gathered the cups and plates from the lamp tables in the living room.

Though she thought of every excuse in the world, she'd decided tonight she had to clear the air. She no longer questioned her feelings for Clint. He was the only man for her, one she wanted to live with forever, and she sensed if she only said the word, he'd be on his knee with a ring. The sparks between them had grown to fire, but they knew the boundaries and kept them. Yet each time together grew more difficult to control.

Clint darted back in, his arms wrapped around his body, a shiver running through him. He opened his arms to her, and she stepped in, feeling the icy chill yet still wanting to warm him. She recalled the verses from the New Testament, Ecclesiastes, if she remembered correctly. "Two are better than one." She now understood the meaning of those words, and even the impact of the scripture as it continued. "If two lie down together, they will keep warm. But how can one keep warm alone?" How many cold nights had she spent longing for real love, a love that was sure, a love that held her close and protected her from harm? The vision shuddered through her body.

"Now you're chilled." Clint kissed her cheek and

unwrapped his arms. "It's time for that hot chocolate I mentioned last night."

"It wasn't you. A thought ran through my mind, that's all."

He frowned. "It couldn't have been a good one. Did my parents do anything to—"

"No. They were wonderful, Clint. I loved meeting them. It's just..." She worked a moment to gather her wits. "Let's sit. Okay?"

Concern knocked the smile from his face, and he studied her a moment before he turned and sank onto the sofa.

"Meeting your parents made me realize how much more you mean to me, more than I've wanted to admit. Your parents are lovely people, and they adore you." She dragged in a breath. "You noticed I became a bit distracted during the evening, and I was sorry about that. I hope I didn't hurt your parents' feelings."

He waved her words away. "It takes more than that to hurt Mom and Dad." He tilted his head, his eyes searching hers. "What are you trying to say. I'm not certain what's bothering you."

"It's not you. It's me. I looked at you with your family and started thinking of my mess of a family, and—"

"I worried about that, Paula. I should have been more sensitive."

"No, I loved seeing it. Actually, seeing all of you made me think of the difference in my life."

She told him about the thoughts that had woven through her mind, the horrors her mother had gone through with the uncle, and she suspected she didn't know half of it. "The more I thought, the more my heart softened, and I began to feel differently. I understand my mother better and can see why loving and trusting was impossible for her. She did the best she could with a limited education, and a life trying to put food in our mouths. She did what she had to. I didn't have to forgive her anymore, because I no longer felt as I did. I only wish I'd realized that earlier."

Clint's eyes were misty as he looked at her. "Those are words that I've longed to hear, Paula. You've grown so much, both in faith and in living. I can't tell you how wonderful that makes me feel."

"The awareness has closed some doors that needed closing. For that I'm grateful."

He nodded, then turned and motioned to the gift she'd given him. "When I said the gift meant so much to me, I meant that, but I meant even more, because—"

"I know. I saw it in your face."

His tense expression softened. "I told you one day you'd read me the same way I read you sometimes." He patted the cushion beside him. "Come here."

"In a minute." Her chest tightened, realizing now she would ruin the beautiful moment. "You're right about my faith growing. I still have much to learn, but I no longer question the reality of the Lord. He's as real to me as the rising sun."

She saw him shift as if he wanted to take her in his arms, but she couldn't. Touching him would only delay what she had to do. "So saying that, I need to get to the serious part of this conversation."

"Serious part?" Tension darkened his face again. "Tell me. What is it?"

"Before you and I go any further in this relationship I have to fill in some holes I left in my story. Holes I'd rather fill with dirt and have them buried forever, but they never will until I am totally open with you." She saw the disappointment grow on his face, but she had to continue.

"You remember when I told you one of my mother's men came after me."

His eyes widened. "Don't tell me he—"

"No. I told you the truth about that." She hesitated, questioning her decision. Then she faced the fact that it had to be told. "But I left out one part. My mother knew what her live-in wanted to do with me, and still she didn't throw him out. That day she'd left us alone, she remembered a comment he'd made before she left, and she realized she couldn't let it happen. She came back and caught him before he…"

Clint's face paled. "Paula…" He opened his mouth but nothing came out until he closed his eyes and began again. "Now I can understand your bad feelings for your mother. I can't even wrap my mind around it. But it doesn't reflect who you are, and even though you lived with that horror, you gave up your job and returned home to care for her. You can't ignore that you followed Jesus's instruction to do to others as you would have them do for you, and, in a way—" he lowered his head "—to love your enemies." He lifted his eyes to hers. "You did that."

"Thank you." Her chest ached with the rehashing of those horrible experiences. Seeing his anguish, she dragged her final admission from the depths of her being, the one that made her sick. "What's even worse is what happened later after that incident."

Clint looked confused. "But the lowlife was gone."

She nodded "He was, but after it happened, the memory lingered in my mind often, and sometimes when I remembered that day, I recalled how warm it felt to have someone hug me." Tears blurred her vision as the memory pierced her. "And I wished he had done more, because then I felt needed and wanted." She swallowed, holding back the sadness that wrought her helpless. Her throat tightened. "That disgusting moment, and I felt wanted. Clint, I was pitiful."

Clint's hands knotted as he shook his head. "No, Paula. Why do you say you're pitiful? We all want to be loved. Expressions of love are gentle touches, embraces, tender kisses. You were a only child."

"I was then, but those same feelings stayed with

me, the longing to be held, to experience being needed and wanting to be loved."

His head lowered, and she knew her words hurt him, but she had to go on.

"After I left home and got my own apartment, occasionally I'd bring guys home." Her eyes shifted from him, but she forced them back, hoping that he would look at her. That somehow he would understand. "And when they left, I felt unclean and even more unloved. I began to see those one-night stands weren't the answer."

Clint lifted his head, his lips squeezed so tightly they looked as if they would have to be pried apart.

She burrowed for strength. "That lasted a few months, and then I met Vic." She dragged in a breath. "And you know about that fiasco. That's all of it, Clint. I've wiped the slate clean."

He didn't speak. All she heard was the walls creaking as they shrank in the icy cold.

"Thanks for being honest." He finally looked at her, but he didn't move.

Aching, she longed for his arms around her, telling her he understood. "Clint, I told you so much before and you insisted I wasn't to blame. I realize this is different since I had choices, but—"

"Paula, don't apologize. I need to think this through. It's a lot to grasp, but I will. Right now, I'd like to let it sink in."

She looked at the empty cushion beside him and

longed to be there, to be in his arms. "Did you want the hot chocolate now?"

He glanced at his watch. "No, it's been a long day, and I need to clean up a bit at home. Get the dishes put away, and…I work tomorrow."

The bottom fell from her heart. "I understand." She managed a nod and rose. "I'll send the cake home with you. The guys might enjoy it." She left the room, forcing herself to get a grip while she found a plastic plate for the rest of the cake and covered it in plastic wrap.

When she returned, he stood by the door, his hand on the knob. "Here you go, and happy birthday."

His head flew up as if startled. "I'll pick up the nativity set another time, if that's okay."

"It's fine."

He turned the knob and then looked at her again. "Thanks for everything."

"You're welcome."

A rush of frigid air swept through the doorway when he pushed open the storm door. He stepped outside and hurried to his car, and she watched him pull away. No blink of lights or a little toot. Nothing as usual when he left, and she sensed this might be what she had feared. The end of a dream that had become real.

After she closed the door, she dropped to the floor, her face in her hand, and wept.

Chapter Fifteen

The engines rolled into the apparatus bay, and Clint slipped to the concrete floor. The scent of smoke clung to his turnout gear. He stripped down to his uniform and joined the others cleaning the gear used at the fire. Following the established routine, his mind drifted to his last talk with Paula.

This time she'd startled him, and he wished it wouldn't have made an impact. He'd heard about her experience with Vic and recognized the guy as a scam artist and a cad, but the one-night stands created pictures in his mind that he couldn't dismiss. Questions jammed his thoughts until nothing else sank in. How easy had it been to bring strangers home to spend the night? How often had it happened? Why had she continued when she'd said she felt unclean and unloved? But the worst question was, could she do this again?

He knew she'd changed and professed her new-found beliefs. He'd watched her grow and gain confidence as a desirable woman. He sensed she understood her past and why she couldn't allow it to control her life, and she'd grown to better understand her mother. Everything positive. He knew her. He read her expressions that often told the real story. He'd witnessed her sorrow for her past. So why did the images flash through his mind?

Would he have preferred not to know? He'd asked himself the question many times since he'd heard her admission. They'd agreed to honesty. That was what she gave him. He saw that it tore her to bits to divulge the past that shamed her so deeply. No one would do that on a whim. She'd struggled with it, and he'd witnessed her pain as she spoke that day.

He longed for a shower to wash off the stench of the fire, and he wished he could wash the stink of his confusion. He'd acted like a jerk, walking away, making an excuse so as to not deal with her confession. If he truly loved her, he would stand by her and not judge.

But he did love her. Nothing could sway the deep emotion that she'd brought out in him. Her vulnerability had captured his attention, her determination had created interest, and stepping into her world had opened his heart. Her wit, her bravery and her gentle nature, despite her past, wove into the kind of woman he could admire and want to spend a lifetime with.

He lowered his head, working on his mask and air tank. His solution. Apologize. But even the word lay limp in his head. Undoing the damage he'd done overwhelmed him.

Devon had looked at him a few times before the fire as if he suspected something had happened, but Devon hadn't asked, and he was grateful. The situation belonged to Paula and him. Only he could resolve it, and he would.

His ring tone vibrated in his pocket, and his first hopeful thought was Paula, but he read his mother's ID. He released a breath and hit the button. He heard her upbeat voice, and he had no intention of worrying her about what had happened.

"We've just come in from fighting a fire."

"Was it bad? I hope no one—"

"The building's gone, but no casualties."

"Phew. Good. Well...I just wanted to tell you your dad and I had a lovely time. We enjoyed meeting Paula, and...we were wondering..."

Here it comes. It took him back to his teen days.

"Wondering if you two have, you know, serious intentions. Your dad and I talked about it on the way home, and we're both enamored with her, and hope you have bigger plans—"

"Mom, yes, I'm crazy about her, but we're taking it slow. Both of us have had a bad relationship, and—"

"Goodness, Clint, that was over three years ago. I'd think you'd be over that by now."

He muzzled a scream. "I am, Mom. Way over

it, but an experience like that still makes a person think. I hope soon we'll—"

"Be engaged. That's it, right?"

It hadn't been what he'd started to say, but getting his mom to hang up meant making her happy, and in truth, that's what he wanted. "That's it."

"Your dad will be as happy as I am. We can't wait to have some grandbabies we can love."

Clint winced, unable to forget Paula's fear of being a mother. Nothing he'd said seemed to change her view of herself. "You and Dad would do a good job with that, Mom, but let's take one step at a time."

She chuckled. "Tell Paula we send our love, and I'll let you go. You sound tired."

"I am. Fighting fires doesn't lend itself to a good time." As soon as the words left his mouth, he wished he'd not said it.

"Rest and take care of yourself. Dad sends his love, too."

"Thanks, Mom. Tell Dad I send my love."

She hesitated but finally disconnected, and he was grateful he hadn't offended her with his crass comment. He adored his parents. He couldn't ask for better, but for some reason, his mom never remembered he'd just turned thirty-eight. Not twenty. He grinned and tucked the cell into his pocket.

He checked the last piece of equipment, and with the job done, he headed for the showers, welcoming the scent of soap and shampoo. As he stripped down, he heard a text message ping on his cell phone, and he tapped the button. Paula's message popped up, and his heart skipped. His eyes swept over the message. Neely was in labor, and Paula was heading for the hospital in a few minutes. He sent up a quick prayer for mother and child and added another for his next talk with Paula, praying the Lord gave him the words to admit he'd been a jerk and to tell her he loved her.

Paula gripped the steering wheel as her car spun out backing from her driveway. They hadn't plowed the latest snowfall and now it had frozen. When she arrived home from work, she'd ground her teeth at the snow blocking her driveway, but she'd barreled through it. Now startled by the quick freeze, she kept her eye on the speedometer as she neared her corner, and calculated the best time to pull out onto Woodward Avenue.

Though stressed by the weather, her spirit lightened each time she thought of Neely and Jon welcoming their new baby into the world. They would make wonderful parents. She'd watched them with Ash and Devon's kids. Observers might think the children had belonged to Neely and Jon.

Her pulse skipped, thinking about her own pleasure in spending time with Kaylee and Joey. Both were funny and filled with cute ways to manipulate doting adults. She'd allowed them to twist her around their fingers on occasion. The thought she wouldn't make a good parent had been filtered with her recent experience. For the first time in her life, she could envision the possibility.

Finally seeing the lane clear, she edged onto Woodward and picked up speed, worrying about the crazies speeding behind her. Her heart stopped as a car skidded toward her. She gripped the wheel and veered left, managing to move into the next lane. She thanked the Lord no other vehicles had blocked her as she steered to safety.

A car zoomed past her, and her chest tightened as she gulped for air. She might have hesitated leaving the house if she'd realized the danger on the highway, but she'd really wanted to be there when the new baby arrived.

Calming herself, she stayed in the new lane. In less than five miles, she had to make a left turn after she passed 13 Mile so this saved her the move later. The traffic became more bold, and a horn tooted behind her. She had nowhere to go, but when she eyed the rearview mirror, her heart flew to her throat. A car sliding sideways was heading for her from behind but instead clipped the car beside her. She clung to the wheel with no control as her car spun and headed into the third lane.

A thud slammed her forward with her heart in her throat, and the crush of metal was followed by a clank from the right. Her head hit the side window. Her sight blurred as a car in front of her spun toward her. Metal crunched. Glass splintered. White blinded her. Then darkness.

* * *

Clint tied his shoes and stood, his thoughts on Neely. He'd listened for the ping of a text message, but none came. He drew in a breath, worrying about Jon and Neely on the slippery highway as they drove to the hospital. No one wanted their baby born in a car.

Driving had been treacherous. While some drivers drove as if on tiptoes, others still considered the roads their own autobahn with no good sense as to the danger they faced. Earlier on the way back to the station after they'd fought the fire, he'd spotted on the shoulder of the road three cars that had either spun out or had had a fender bender. Nothing life threatening, but a good warning to passing traffic.

He stepped into the hallway and faltered as the siren sounded again, but this time the loudspeaker announced a four-car accident on North Woodward and 9 Mile Road. His shoulders drooped, knowing the crew would face another long night.

Joining the others, he retraced his steps to the bunker room and found himself again tugging on his turnout gear and climbing into the rig as they rolled outside, the siren whooping to warn traffic. Woodward Avenue, though salted, continued to be slippery, the ice having melted and then frozen again, leaving traffic creeping. The urgency of the sirens sent many to the shoulder where they waited for the engine and rescue unit to pass.

The short trip took forever, and as they arrived,

police where already setting up barricades and detouring traffic down clogged side streets. Ahead he could see the tangle of the four-car pileup, and as they drew closer, his heart stood still as terror surged through his limbs. "Oh, dear Lord, no."

Sal's head swiveled toward him. "What is it?"

"That's Paula's car."

Sal shook his head. "Are you sure? It can't be?"

"It is." He craned his neck, positive the vehicle was hers, but managed to contain his growing fear. He could never forget he was a firefighter. "Neely's in labor, and Paula was on her way to Beaumont."

Fighting for the control he needed in emergencies, he jumped from the engine when it came to a full stop and raced to the car pinned in between the three others. Drivers from two of the vehicles stood beside the road, talking to police, while two officers attempted to get to the center of the pileup.

His stomach knotted as he stepped onto the rear bumper, climbed over the trunk to the top of the car and leaned over to look through the windshield. Blood rolled down her face, and he gasped. "Paula." His voice thrummed in his ears, but she didn't move. "Paula." She lay unconscious against the driver's door, the white airbags draped around her. Fear surged as he searched for evidence of life, but a faint rise of her chest gave him hope.

"She's unconscious and bleeding from the head, but alive."

The crew surrounded the scene, assessing the damage and the best way to get to her car.

He spotted the only safe way. "Access her through the passenger door. Get someone to move that van," he yelled over his shoulder, knowing any other way of moving her would be more dangerous for her.

Two of his pals had already appeared with the rescue tools—cutters and spreaders—the Jaws of Life, which lived up to its name. Though longing to stay near her, he retraced his path and slid from the car while the men strategized their next move.

Relief spread through him as a tow truck appeared and pulled in front of the tangle. The driver lined up with the van blocking Paula's passenger-side door. The driver hooked the winch cable to the van's engine cradle, climbed into the wrecker and rolled the vehicle forward.

Grasping the spreader, Clint darted back to the car and attacked the passenger door, inserting the narrow tip between the door and frame before he used the hydraulic pressure to separate them. His prayer rose that the Lord give him a chance to tell Paula he loved her.

The crunch of metal and screech of hinges breaking loose resounded in his ears.

The door budged, and his heart hammered as the new access into her front seat would allow him to rescue Paula. With a thud, the door dangled from a single hinge and then struck the ground.

Paula remained unmoving, and he prayed. He

then shifted away to give the paramedics room to do their job. As they immobilized her neck with a cervical collar and maneuvered her body onto a stretcher, viselike fear squeezed air from his lungs.

Before they lifted her into the ambulance, he hurried to her side, heart pounding, and touched her cheek. His fingers warmed, and hope soared. With his voice only a whisper, he spoke her name, but she didn't react. When the technician encouraged him to move away, he bent to her ear once more. "I love you, Paula."

As the EMT's siren hooted, he held his breath, relieved yet still worried. He returned to his crew, his feet slipping on the ice. He assisted with the hoses they were using to wash away gasoline that had escaped from a crushed gas tank. He lifted his eyes again and watched the taillights of the ambulance vanishing in the distance and felt his heart go with them.

Paula forced her eyes open once more, her vision still blurred, and she closed them again, wanting only to sleep. She'd awakened earlier and tried to wrap her head around the accident, but a nurse appeared, asking questions she couldn't answer and taking her vital signs. She tried to learn what happened when she arrived, but the nurse quieted her and listened to her pulse and heartbeat. Before she could inquire again, the woman turned and left, leaving her uncertain.

Alone, the vague recollection clotted in her mind as she grappled to recall bits and pieces of what had happened. At first she couldn't remember where she'd been going, and then it came to her. Neely had been in labor. Besides confusion, disappointment seeped through her. She'd longed to be there and hear the good news when it happened.

She gazed at the wall clock but had no reference to make sense whether it was day or night. How much time had passed since she'd been admitted escaped her. Had it been an hour, a day, two days? She had no way of knowing until she asked someone who would answer her. Her head throbbed and, concerned, she raised her hand to her forehead and touched a bandage on her hairline.

Wanting someone to appear who could answer her questions, she tried to open her eyes again. Her eyelids felt glued closed, and though she willed them to open, she failed at the attempt.

A sound alerted her to someone near the bed, and a shadow darkened her closed eyelids. "Nurse, how long have I been here?"

"Three hours."

Lips pressed against her cheek, and her heart skipped. "Clint?"

His eyes widened. "What?"

"Do you know anything about Neely? Is she—"

"She's the mother of a strapping baby boy."

Her heart swelled. "And they're both all right? Everything's fine?"

They're great. Perfect."

"Jon must be thrilled." She caught herself. "And Neely, too. What am I thinking?"

"You're thinking that Jon has someone to carry his last name." He touched her cheek and drew his finger to her lips.

"I wanted to be there. I'm happy for them but disappointed."

Clint brushed his palm across her arm. "As soon as they let you up, we'll go to the nursery, and you can see him for yourself. How's that?"

Anxious, she couldn't stop now. "Go to the desk and ask if we can go. Please."

He shook his head. "You have to use good sense. You have a concussion. Not serious but moderate. Still, they have to take precautions."

"A concussion?" First time for everything. "What does that mean?"

"They'll explain it when the doctor comes. He's supposed to be here soon. Be grateful it wasn't more serious. You could be... You've just been in a bad accident."

Dead. She suspected that's what he started to say. "I know I was in an accident, but what happened? Do you know?"

"Four-car pileup. Yours was lodged between two other vehicles and another had spun out and was in front of you."

"And my car's totaled, isn't it?" She studied his face, seeing the answer. "What will I do now?"

Clint patted her arm, his eyes questioning. "Don't worry about that now. I'm on it."

She lowered her head, sorry she sounded so ungrateful. "I know I should be happy to be alive, and I am." Overwhelmed, she recoiled. "But how can I get to work and—"

"Paula, do you think I would let that happen? You'll have a car. Promise."

She managed to lift her chin and witnessed the worried look on his face. Furrows etched his brow, and dark rings circled his eyes. Frustrated with herself, she gave a nod. "Thank you."

Silence settled over them, but she still had so many questions. "How did you hear about the accident?"

"We're called for all bad accidents." He shook his head as if clearing his thoughts. "My heart stopped when I saw your car. I had so much to say to you. So many things I wanted to apologize for…and all I kept thinking about was what a jerk I'd been."

Her eyes closed again, remembering the last time they'd spoken. She'd been heartbroken. Wounded. But she understood. "Clint, let's not discuss it now. You're exhausted. Anyway, it's not important anymore. It happened, and there's nothing—"

"Yes, there is. There's a lot I can do. First, I'm asking for your forgiveness. The whole conversation startled me. I couldn't imagine your living like—"

"I can't imagine it either anymore, but it's true. It's natural you would wonder if I could revert to that lifestyle again. I might ask myself the same question of you in a similar situation, except…" She drew in a breath, trying to imagine it. "Except I know you could never be that kind of person. Never."

"You can't, either, Paula I know that."

"I understand your concern. You trusted Elise, offering her a life of companionship, security and love, and she turned her back on it." She slipped her hand across the rough sheet and touched his. "You trusted her, and for what? Why would you trust me when you saw evidence that I might do the same."

"But I never saw evidence of that, Paula. I know you hate that part of your life. You were unhappy when I first met you even though you could laugh and joke. I saw the vulnerability in your eyes. That's what I first loved about you."

Trying to shift her head higher, it spun, and she sank back. "How could you love a person for that?"

He searched her eyes, and he wove his fingers with hers. "I said it is what I first loved about you."

Clint meant something more, but her fogged mind couldn't find it.

"You look puzzled." He grinned.

Her free hand shifted to her forehead. "I am."

"Now I just plain old love you, Paula. All of you." He leaned closer his lips nearing hers. "With all my heart."

His lips pressed hers, and she sailed away, enveloped in the dreams she'd had of finding her own

Prince Charming. She'd found him soon after they'd met, though she'd refused to admit it, but today he'd found her. "I love you, too, Clint, and I will forever."

Chapter Sixteen

Clint hit the button beneath the tree, and the Christmas lights glowed.

"It's pretty." She rose and slipped her arms around his waist. "It's small and doesn't smell of pine, but I'm burning a pine candle, and it's still perfect."

"Just like you." He drew her closer and kissed her hair. "You're small and you don't smell like pine, either, but you're still perfect." He lifted her finger and gazed at the diamond glinting brighter than the Christmas lights. "I love you, Paula."

"I love you, too. You make my life—" She jerked back, her hand flying to her mouth. "I forgot." She darted from his arms and headed down the hall.

"What?" He followed her, trying to make sense out of her yell. He assumed she was worried about the food for the family get-together. "Everything's fine, Paula. You have dessert, mulled cider and coffee. That's plenty for Christmas Eve. It's not Christmas Day yet."

She reappeared, holding a store bag from Shine. "The handblown Christmas balls."

He nodded. "I didn't have time to put them on, and then we had our..."

She didn't want to be reminded of that day. "I'm not blaming you, but the family's coming and I want them to see how beautiful they are."

He took the sack from her, and together they hung them around the tree, each in a spot that caught the glow of the clear lights. "I have to admit, they are beautiful."

She grinned. "And they're the first Christmas present you bought me. The second was the new car."

"True," he said, drawing her close again, but this time touching her lips with his, a kiss that was only the taste of things to come.

The doorbell chimed, and she shifted back again and ran to the door. He waited and heard her outburst of pleasure.

Paula's voice sailed from the doorway. "Let me hold him while you take off your coat." She drifted from the foyer with baby Nicholas cuddled in her arms. He held his breath, amazed at the desire that rose inside him. "You look good that way."

She grinned and ambled toward him. "Did I tell you I changed my mind?"

He tilted his head, unsure of how to respond. "About what?"

"I'd make a great mother. I know—"

"You will." Neely stepped from the foyer, a smile brightening her face. "I never doubted you would."

Jon finished hanging the coats, and before he joined them, the door opened again, and Devon and Ashley strode in followed by Uncle Fred and his lady friend, Alice.

After kisses, hugs and greetings all around, Paula returned the baby to Neely and headed for the kitchen to set up the treats while he struggled to hold back their news and monitor his smile, which was ready to burst. "Let me hug that baby." He opened his arms and nestled the boy to his chest. "Hello there, Nick. What do you think of your first Christmas?"

Jon chuckled. "I know he'll be a brilliant boy, but if he answers you, wow."

The others laughed as they found seats, and Paula returned to the room, trying to control her happiness. "I don't recall anyone else in the family named Nick. Who'd you name him after?"

Jon shook his head and gestured toward Neely, a grin on his face. "Let his mommy tell you."

Neely gazed at her new son. "We knew he would be a Christmas baby or close to it so we began thinking of names. For a girl, we considered Noel, Holly, Ivy, even Joy, but we went blank on a boy's name. Noel might work but I associate that with a girl, so I got the idea to call him Nicholas after Saint Nicholas."

Clint spurted a laugh. "You mean Santa Claus?"

"That was her thinking." Jon rested his arm around her shoulder. "And I liked it. St. Nicholas was the spirit of Christmas and a very strong believer. He decided to live a life like Christ."

"I didn't know that." Clint had second thoughts about his humor. "I think it's a good choice."

Everyone agreed, and baby Nicholas passed from Clint to Ashley, whose face glowed. "This is a good time to let you all know that, though this isn't official, Devon and I are going to have our own little one to name soon."

Arms flew around their necks in a chaotic jumble of loved ones, and when they settled down after calculating June as the date for the new baby's arrival, Paula announced it was time for snacks and dessert.

"But first." Clint scanned the group, seeing their attentive faces. "I've asked Paula to marry me, and she said yes."

Paula extended her hand, flashing her engagement ring at the family craning their necks to see.

"It's beautiful." Ashley's words were covered by Neely's "Gorgeous." The cousins nearly knocked Paula to the ground with their exuberance.

Fred sidled between his daughters and slipped his arms around them. "You girls have made me proud." He beckoned to Paula. "I need another arm." He managed to squeeze her into the hug. "You've all found wonderful men to make your lives complete. I know how important that is." He shifted his focus to Paula. "You remember our discussion about two are better than one." A serious expression touched his face as he scanned the group. "That's a biblical truth. I pray every day for your lives to be filled with joy, peace and love, and I've decided to do the same. Alice and I will be married after the new year, and—"

The utter silence broke into cheers and embraces. Alice hugged the girls, tears glowing in her eyes. "I'm blessed to have you all as part of my family."

The surprises filled the room with conversation, but once sated with congratulations and more details, they settled around in the dining room to enjoy the crackers, meat and cheese spread along with the large tray of Christmas cookies Paula had baked.

Clint leaned over and kissed her cheek, amazed at the changes she'd made in his life and hers. The lovely woman hiding her sorrow beneath her sharp wit while changing her past to a beautiful future. He thanked the Lord daily for the gift.

When everyone's bellies were full and they'd admired the handblown balls on the Christmas tree, they bound up in their winter coats, wrapped baby Nick in warm blankets and said their goodbyes until the Christmas Day worship service in the morning. Clint's chest expanded with a new joy he'd only begun to accept. Life couldn't be any more complete than this.

Paula stood in the doorway, watching her family drive home. A lump formed in her throat seeing their happiness for Clint and her when they'd announced their upcoming marriage. Good news rained like spring showers, and it reminded her of the Good News of Christmas, the child born in a lowly stable and swaddled in a manger. Despite her lack of faith, God had been a true Father to her, guiding her without her knowing and handing her a life she had never imagined.

She lifted her eyes to Clint, who'd joined her at the door, and when she closed it and turned toward him, he took her into his arms with a kiss that completed her joy.

"Everyone enjoyed themselves, I think."

He rested his cheek against hers. "No doubt at all. And so many surprises."

She nodded, envisioning the glow in the room as each shared their wonderful news. "For the first time in my life, I have a real family. Not real sisters, but as close to it as a person can get. Sort of a sisterhood. A wholeness I've never known, and you are a huge part of it, Clint."

His hand slipped upward and his fingers brushed through her hair. "We've both done it, Paula. I rescued you, and you rescued me."

Their eyes connected in a look that made them smile.

Paula recognized their thoughts were the same. "And we were both rescued in another way."

He nodded. "By the birth we celebrate now. A savior."

She snuggled closer and kissed his lips, knowing that she had a lifetime of kisses waiting for him.

He held her fast. "It won't be long, and I can call you Mrs. Donatelli. The thought makes my pulse go crazy."

"And I'm giving up a nice simple name that is easy to say. Paula Reynolds." She raised her shoulders and let them drop. "Oh, well, Donatelli has a much better ring, don't you think?" She held up her hand adorned with her engagement ring.

"Absolutely."

As his lips touched hers, her pulse soared, and she greeted him with a kiss so deep and joyful they both lost their breath. She'd heard of love and kisses like they shared, but it took the Lord's guidance and blessing to make it an amazing reality.

* * * * *

Paula's Scrumptious Poppy-Seed Cake

This cake has been in my family for years. The recipe was given to me by my sister many years ago, and we've all loved it. Though it looks a bit more complicated than Paula thought, it's well worth the time, and it's really not that complicated. I serve it with a whipped topping, but ice cream is good, too, or just plain. It's moist and luscious.

¾ pound margarine or butter (3 sticks)
1½ cups of sugar
4 egg yolks (save egg whites for later)
2 ounces (½ cup) of poppy seeds
1 cup of sour cream
1 tsp baking soda
2 cups flour
3 tsps vanilla
4 egg whites beaten to stiff peaks

Mix margarine, sugar, yolks and poppy seeds well. Stir baking soda with sour cream until dissolved. Stir into mixture. Add flour and vanilla. Mix well.

Beat egg whites to stiff peaks using a metal or glass bowl (avoid plastic) and fold into the batter.

Place batter into a greaseless tube pan and bake at 350°F degrees for 1 hour. Invert pan to cool.

Enjoy!

Dear Reader,

I hope you've enjoyed the final novel in the Sisters series. You met Neely in *Her Valentine Hero* and Ashley in *The Firefighter's New Family*. Here you met Paula, the cousin they treated like a sister. Paula was raised in a loveless life and longing for real love. Many of us grew up in a loving family, but many are raised by people who are unable to care for themselves let alone children. The heartbreaking result is an adult who must overcome a variety of warped perceptions and values.

Clint's loving family guided his morals and values, but his error was choosing the wrong marriage partner. Paula helped him see the problem may not have been his fault but the woman he chose. Paula suffered from a loveless childhood with a role model who twisted her view of love and faith. Clint's guidance helped her learn to lean on the Lord and not herself.

Sometimes we face problems that seem hopeless. With warped experiences, past or present, we are misled in resolving our difficulties. We think God doesn't care or we don't see Him at all. Once we feel the Lord's loving arms around us, we can lay our burdens at His feet. I pray we all learn to lean on His abiding love. Blessings.

Gail Gaymer Martin

Questions for Discussion

1. What kind of family relationships have you seen in your own family, friends or neighbors? Do any remind you of Paula's family, and if so, what are they?

2. What would life be like if you had to raise a child (or children) alone after your mate walked out on you? Feelings?

3. Does Clint's family seem realistic? What did you like or not like about his mother and father?

4. Paula wanted to disassociate herself from her past. Is that possible? Why or why not?

5. How would your life change if you didn't believe in God?

6. How does the Bible verse assigned to this novel relate to the story? 1 John 1: 7-9 "But if you walk in the light, we have fellowship with one another, and the blood of Jesus, His Son, purifies us from all sin."

7. Do you agree with Clint that "love your enemy"

can be attributed to Paula's relationship with her mother?

8. In what way did Ashley, Neely and their dad, Fred, help her heal?

9. Can people grow and change as Paula did? Was this realistic in the novel and why?

10. At first Paula thought lacking a motherly role model would affect her ability to be a good parent. What do you think about this and why?

11. Did you find any surprises in the story that you hadn't expected? Did some help you to understand Paula's problem more clearly?

12. Did you learn anything new about firefighters and their work?

13. If you read all three novels in the series, did you enjoy the ending? What elements helped you envision the individuals' futures?

14. Did you enjoy the book? Why or why not? Which of the three novels in the series did you enjoy the most and why?

LARGER-PRINT BOOKS!

GET 2 FREE
LARGER-PRINT NOVELS
PLUS 2 FREE
MYSTERY GIFTS

Love Inspired®
SUSPENSE
RIVETING INSPIRATIONAL ROMANCE

Larger-print novels are now available...

YES! Please send me 2 FREE LARGER-PRINT Love Inspired® Suspense novels and my 2 FREE mystery gifts (gifts are worth about $10). After receiving them, if I don't wish to receive any more books, I can return the shipping statement marked "cancel." If I don't cancel, I will receive 4 brand-new novels every month and be billed just $5.24 per book in the U.S. or $5.74 per book in Canada. That's a savings of at least 23% off the cover price. It's quite a bargain! Shipping and handling is just 50¢ per book in the U.S. and 75¢ per book in Canada.* I understand that accepting the 2 free books and gifts places me under no obligation to buy anything. I can always return a shipment and cancel at any time. Even if I never buy another book, the two free books and gifts are mine to keep forever.

110/310 IDN F5CC

Name	(PLEASE PRINT)	
Address		Apt. #
City	State/Prov.	Zip/Postal Code

Signature (if under 18, a parent or guardian must sign)

Mail to the **Harlequin® Reader Service:**
IN U.S.A.: P.O. Box 1867, Buffalo, NY 14240-1867
IN CANADA: P.O. Box 609, Fort Erie, Ontario L2A 5X3

**Are you a current subscriber to Love Inspired Suspense books
and want to receive the larger-print edition?
Call 1-800-873-8635 or visit www.ReaderService.com.**

* Terms and prices subject to change without notice. Prices do not include applicable taxes. Sales tax applicable in N.Y. Canadian residents will be charged applicable taxes. Offer not valid in Quebec. This offer is limited to one order per household. Not valid for current subscribers to Love Inspired Suspense larger-print books. All orders subject to credit approval. Credit or debit balances in a customer's account(s) may be offset by any other outstanding balance owed by or to the customer. Please allow 4 to 6 weeks for delivery. Offer available while quantities last.

Your Privacy—The Harlequin® Reader Service is committed to protecting your privacy. Our Privacy Policy is available online at www.ReaderService.com or upon request from the Harlequin Reader Service.

We make a portion of our mailing list available to reputable third parties that offer products we believe may interest you. If you prefer that we not exchange your name with third parties, or if you wish to clarify or modify your communication preferences, please visit us at www.ReaderService.com/consumerschoice or write to us at Harlequin Reader Service Preference Service, P.O. Box 9062, Buffalo, NY 14269. Include your complete name and address.

LISLPDIR13R

REQUEST YOUR FREE BOOKS!
2 FREE WHOLESOME ROMANCE NOVELS
IN LARGER PRINT
PLUS 2
FREE
MYSTERY GIFTS

☀☀☀☀☀☀☀☀☀☀☀☀☀☀☀☀☀☀☀☀☀☀☀

HEARTWARMING™

☀☀☀☀☀☀☀☀☀☀☀☀☀☀☀☀☀☀☀☀☀☀☀

Wholesome, tender romances

YES! Please send me 2 FREE Harlequin® Heartwarming Larger-Print novels and my 2 FREE mystery gifts (gifts worth about $10). After receiving them, if I don't wish to receive any more books, I can return the shipping statement marked "cancel." If I don't cancel, I will receive 4 brand-new larger-print novels every month and be billed just $4.99 per book in the U.S. or $5.74 per book in Canada. That's a savings of at least 23% off the cover price. It's quite a bargain! Shipping and handling is just 50¢ per book in the U.S. and 75¢ per book in Canada.* I understand that accepting the 2 free books and gifts places me under no obligation to buy anything. I can always return a shipment and cancel at any time. Even if I never buy another book, the two free books and gifts are mine to keep forever.

161/361 IDN F47N

Name   (PLEASE PRINT)

Address   Apt. #

City   State/Prov.   Zip/Postal Code

Signature (if under 18, a parent or guardian must sign)

Mail to the **Harlequin® Reader Service:**
IN U.S.A.: P.O. Box 1867, Buffalo, NY 14240-1867
IN CANADA: P.O. Box 609, Fort Erie, Ontario L2A 5X3

* Terms and prices subject to change without notice. Prices do not include applicable taxes. Sales tax applicable in N.Y. Canadian residents will be charged applicable taxes. Offer not valid in Quebec. This offer is limited to one order per household. Not valid for current subscribers to Harlequin Heartwarming larger-print books. All orders subject to credit approval. Credit or debit balances in a customer's account(s) may be offset by any other outstanding balance owed by or to the customer. Please allow 4 to 6 weeks for delivery. Offer available while quantities last.

Your Privacy—The Harlequin® Reader Service is committed to protecting your privacy. Our Privacy Policy is available online at www.ReaderService.com or upon request from the Harlequin Reader Service.

We make a portion of our mailing list available to reputable third parties that offer products we believe may interest you. If you prefer that we not exchange your name with third parties, or if you wish to clarify or modify your communication preferences, please visit us at www.ReaderService.com/consumerchoice or write to us at Harlequin Reader Service Preference Service, P.O. Box 9062, Buffalo, NY 14269. Include your complete name and address.

HWDIR13R

Reader Service.com

Manage your account online!

- Review your order history
- Manage your payments
- Update your address

---

*We've designed
the Harlequin® Reader Service
website just for you.*

Enjoy all the features!

- Reader excerpts from any series
- Respond to mailings and
  special monthly offers
- Discover new series available to you
- Browse the Bonus Bucks catalog
- Share your feedback

Visit us at:

ReaderService.com

10/27/17